THE INN ON JERICHO ROAD

THE INN ON JERICHO ROAD

The story of the Good Samaritan retold by
STAN ESCOTT

PALMETTO
P U B L I S H I N G
Charleston, SC
www.PalmettoPublishing.com

Copyright © 2024 by Stan Escott

All rights reserved

No portion of this book may be reproduced, stored in a retrieval system, or transmitted in any form by any means–electronic, mechanical, photocopy, recording, or other–except for brief quotations in printed reviews, without prior permission of the author.

Hardcover ISBN: 979-8-8229-5698-8
Paperback ISBN: 979-8-8229-5699-5
eBook ISBN: 979-8-8229-5700-8

Witness: One who has experienced an event and testifies to the truth.
Merriam-Webster Dictionary

And he said, "He who showed mercy on him." Then Jesus said to him, "Go and do likewise." Luke 10:37

DEDICATION

Barbara Elaine Speicher

Strong is the soul, and wise and beautiful:
The seeds of her faith and love are with us still.

By Matthew Arnold

This book is dedicated to Barbara Speicher, loving wife, mother, a calm gentle hero, and patient follower of our Lord. Barbara personified all those who walk with us through this life, helpers that shape us more closely into God's purpose. Without that lover, that friend, that partner, that special person in our lives, we would not live out our days as dedicated followers of our Lord. Therefore, this book honors all those who follow our Lord's admonition to 'go and do likewise'.

TABLE OF CONTENTS

Prologue		xi
Chapter 1	The Samaritan	1
Chapter 2	Samaria?	4
Chapter 3	Jesus at the Well	6
Chapter 4	An Amazing Time	11
Chapter 5	The Merchant	13
Chapter 6	Reconciliation	16
Chapter 7	The Journey	19
Chapter 8	Afula	23
Chapter 9	A Girl Alone	27
Chapter 10	Schooling Mara	30
Chapter 11	Scythopolis	33
Chapter 12	Stories Told	37
Chapter 13	Until I See Proof	40
Chapter 14	Conflict Brewing	45
Chapter 15	Old-School vs.??	49
Chapter 16	Gadara	53
Chapter 17	A Miracle?	57
Chapter 18	A Trick!	63
Chapter 19	Change of Plans	66
Chapter 20	Trouble	68
Chapter 21	A Perfect Day	72
Chapter 22	On To Jericho	75
Chapter 23	Matthias	80
Chapter 24	Did It Really Happen?	84
Chapter 25	Jericho Road	86
Chapter 26	Who Is My Neighbor?	88
Chapter 27	But God…	91
Chapter 28	Not At My Inn!	94

Chapter 29	Doing Likewise	98
Chapter 30	To Trust or Not	102
Chapter 31	Yosef's Story	105
Chapter 32	Shimon Returns	107
Chapter 33	The Story Continues	113
Chapter 34	Conflicted	118
Chapter 35	The Crucifixion	121
Chapter 36	Back In the Temple?	124
Chapter 37	Shared Conflicts	126
Chapter 38	What Am I To Think?	129
Chapter 39	It's God's Love	132
Chapter 40	Time To Go	136
Chapter 41	Naomi's Return	140
Chapter 42	Yosef's Dilemma	144
Chapter 43	Shimon in Bethany	147
Chapter 44	I Am The Way	151
Chapter 45	The Sadducee and the Disciple	154
Chapter 46	Two Masters?	158
Chapter 47	Sychar	161
Chapter 48	Why Is He Here?	166
Chapter 49	Dreidels and Raisons	169
Chapter 50	Visitors	171
Chapter 51	Going Home	174
Chapter 52	God's Plan	176

Appendix A ··· 179
Appendix B ··· 188
Appendix C ··· 189
Acknowledgements ·· 191
About the Author: ·· 193

PROLOGUE

The deep division between the people of Samaria and the Jews of Judea was long entrenched and, over the centuries, had been passed from one generation to the next. Some believed that the animosity began more than five-hundred years before, a time when Samaria was known as a refuge, a hiding place for criminals and Great Sea pirates.

Samaria had always been a mix of races, ethnicities, and beliefs that ranged from idol worship to the worship of God on Mount Gerizim. Samaritans rejected the Jewish insistence that God is worshiped only in the Temple in Jerusalem, which inflamed the Jews. Many of the Psalms, especially those written by David, inflamed the Samaritan followers of their Golden Calf. They singled out the scroll that declares *"Our (Jewish) God is in heaven; he does whatever pleases him. But their idols are silver and gold, made by human hands. They have mouths, but cannot speak, eyes, but cannot see. They have ears, but cannot hear, noses, but cannot smell."* [Psalm 115:3-6]

Forgiveness was not a part of the lexicon for either Jew or Samaritan. Whatever the reasons, the hatred and distrust persisted and was a chasm between them. Frightening stories of distrust, danger, and disaster abound among both peoples.

Jews avoided contact with Samaritans, viewed them as cursed, demon-possessed, and dangerous. Samaritans, for their part, had no dealings with Jews, except in the marketplace. And so, the separation between the two peoples continued, perpetuated by unfounded rumor, myth, and legend.

Then, quietly, unexpectedly, something, at first undefined, occurred, it's influence unrecognized, yet it produced altered thinking, which, over time, caused changes in behavior.

The influence grew so powerful that over the years its impact spread throughout Samaria and Judea, along trade routes, the River Jordan Valley, and continued on, century after century, touching and changing one life after another. The small influence became a revelation, causing wars to be fought and lives to be lost, but the movement continued to build.

And there, along the rough and dangerous Jericho Road, at a simple Inn, a waystation for travelers, four lives, driven by divergent circumstance, were conjoined, unified, and changed. Four lives: a young girl with a sad history, saved from begging and now employed at the

Inn. An arrogant Sadducee, member of the Sanhedrin, ruling council of the temple in Jerusalem, whose experience fueled his doubts and brought change in his life. A tough-minded, unbending merchant from Samaria, selling his specialty wares in marketplaces along the Jordan River, whose skepticism led to blessings. An Innkeeper, prejudiced, working hard to keep the Inn open, changed by the lives of those around him. Four lives, each contributing to the other's spiritual growth and strength.

As each found their way through change in thought and behavior, their outreach to others broadened, even through difficult times, and so the blessings multiplied.

Chapter 1

THE SAMARITAN

Tirzah, Samaria, early morning. The shouting had gone on long enough that neighbors on this side street were getting concerned. Two men, arguing over a transaction that had gone sour. Accusations, back and forth, of cheating, theft, and false promises. Followed by "buyer beware" and "that's a lie!" said loud enough to be heard down the street, where more neighbors had gathered outside their shops.

Finally, Shimon, the merchant, yelled, "Get out of my shop, and don't come back!"

"Don't you worry about that," came the heated reply. "I should've paid attention to my friends who cautioned me about being your friend, let alone buying anything in your shop! They were right in calling you stubborn and as dishonest as the Jews, who at least have the sense not to shop here. I defended you before, but never again!"

"I said, get out!" the merchant yelled, slamming the door. Then silence.

Neighbors watched the man, noticeably upset, leave the merchant's store and storm down the street. They breathed a sigh of relief and returned to their shops. This was not the first time there had been an angry outburst from their neighbor.

Shimon had quite a reputation, deserved or not, of being dishonest and of overpricing goods. Some wondered how he stayed in business, while others knew that his semi-annual journeys to markets along the Jordan had been most lucrative and kept his shop open.

Inside the shop, the merchant sat behind the counter. He was shaken, tears in his eyes. He had just ordered Nahman from his shop. Nahman, who had been a good friend for years. They were like brothers. They had grown up together and supported one another through times of stress and adversity. He was a friend he could always count on. But now?

For long minutes, he wrestled with himself. *Why had I gotten so angry? Who am I angry at? Me! The bad faith was mine. I should have told Nahman he was right, and I needed to change things. Pride. My bullheaded, stupid pride! To hear the truth from one you respected, no, loved, was hard. Especially when you agreed!*

He replayed the conversation that had triggered the eruption: Nahman had calmly pointed out that with the quality of customers Shimon's shop was now attracting, it would be to his advantage to include a wider range of quality goods, at true value. Again, Shimon thought, *why had I gotten so angry? He told me what I was thinking, what I was feeling guilty about, to be honest. Of course, Nahman was right, but it stung me to hear it from someone who is so important in my life.*

Shimon was calm now and thinking more clearly. It wasn't just this clash with Nahman that unhinged him so. His recent market journey to the Jordan had been a real disappointment and weighed heavily on his mind. There weren't many customers, and some of the goods that he took on that trip are now on the shelves, here, in his shop.

Still there was something else. Those stories he had been hearing for the past year bothered him, stories about a rabbi—or was he a carpenter? He shook his head at the memories. *A little girl near death, healed by a carpenter? Seriously? Can you imagine? How about turning water into wine? Hah! I'd like to see the carpenter do that!*

He sighed, looked around his shop and saw that some of the shelves were getting a bit empty. He would soon have to restock. That meant an extra trip to the Port of Caesarea, and the Bizarre on the wharf. He had hoped that he could delay that until closer to his next market journey. But, no, he would need to go soon. He thought, again, about the encounter with his friend. Just to have something to do to calm his mind, he took out the broom and started sweeping.

Shimon thought about what he would need to purchase for the shop and realized that there was hardly any difference in the goods that he purchased for his shop and the more expensive, better-quality goods he took with him on his journeys. *Why should there be a difference?* he thought. *It made sense for the shop to carry the same goods he sold on his market journeys.*

Maybe I should upgrade all the goods sold here and at those markets. Then a thought that almost made him laugh out loud: *Isn't that exactly the point that Nahman had made, the comment that I got so defensive about? What a foolish man I am. Why was I so defensive? Guilt and pride!*

He had to smile when he thought how this latest outburst served to inform his neighbors that he was back in town, bad mood, and all. *Why am I finding humor in any of this? Because it is ridiculous, and the truth is, there are times when I'm ridiculous!* he thought with a chuckle. *And Nahman knows that, and he was still my friend.*

Nahman! He had much to do, but first, and most important, he needed to go to Nahman, apologize to him. Ask for forgiveness for his outburst. Confess that his friend was right. He knew this would be one of the hardest things he had ever done, but that friendship, if it could be restored, was much too important.

Chapter 2

SAMARIA?

Thirty-five miles south of Tirzah, in Jerusalem, Judea, the first light of dawn was reflecting a rosy-golden glow off the sandstone of the massive and ornate walls of the Damascus Gate. Morning prayers were completed. The city was waking.

A small group of men made their way out of the city, through the Gate, beginning their journey toward Capernaum. They had gone but a short distance when, their leader, Jesus, from the village of Nazareth, pointed them west, into Samaria, explaining that he needed to speak to some of the residents.

The group was stunned. Samaria? They looked at one another. As Jews, they wanted no part of Samaria. Throughout their lives, they had always avoided the area. Now Jesus was leading them into the heart of it? They had only been with Jesus a few months, and this was the first traveling they had done with him. Now they were worried. They grumbled among themselves but said nothing to him and followed.

As expected, the pathway had little traffic. Few people traveled between Judea and Samaria because of the fear that both regions felt toward one another. It was fear based on mythology and tales, with little relevance to the present day. But still, it persisted.

It was the seventh watch, the highest temperature of the day, when the group arrived at Jacob's well, between the towns of Shechem and Sychar, eleven miles from Jerusalem. They were hungry, and the disciples continued into town for food, while Jesus remained at the well, waiting for the person he knew would be along soon.

At the same time, in the village of Sychar, a Samaritan woman was leaving her home, with a jar on her shoulder, to get water from the well. She was middle-aged, wearing a long flowing dress and head-covering. Her face bore the unmistakable evidence of a hard life, a life of stress and loss. She chose to suffer the mid-day heat to avoid contact with other women of the town. In truth, it was mutual. They avoided her, a woman rumored to have a soiled reputation. Just that thought angered her, had they only known what her life had been like.

She paused as she approached the well. *What is that man doing here?* she asked herself. *Most unusual, a man alone. What should I do? Could he be a rabbi? Most assuredly, he's a Jew. What is a Jew doing here? That's just great! I'm just not up to dealing with another man.* But, after some thought, she resolved to draw her water, as quickly as she could, then return to town. She stepped to the well, lowered her jar, setting it next to the well. Then she pulled down the draw-rope to lower the levered shadoof into the water.

Chapter 3
JESUS AT THE WELL

Jesus was saying something, just as the Samaritan woman had raised the shadoof and was starting to fill her jar. She kept her attention on her jar, but thoughts filled her mind. *Did he just speak to me? Why would he do that? Clearly, he is not a Samaritan. What did he say? A drink? Yes, he asked me for a drink. Do I answer? I can't ignore him. I don't want any trouble. This is not good!*

Nevertheless, she went about the task of filling her jar. Then she gave him a drink of water. It was then that she decided to challenge him, saying, "Why are you asking me, a Samaritan woman, for anything? Why are you even talking to me?"

The man smiled but said nothing.

She was puzzled at his silence, but after a time, she continued, "Who are you? I can tell you're not from here. I would guess you are from Galilee or Judea. That would make you a Jew. Are you a Jew?"

Jesus smiled at her boldness, then answered, "You could say that Photini. I don't live in Samaria, but since I have a house in Capernaum, you would say I am from Galilee. People call me Jesus."

The woman was alarmed! *He called me by my name! How could he know that? I've never seen him before. A stranger. A Jew no less, knowing my name!* She didn't know what to think about this stranger, yet she didn't feel threatened.

Finally, she said, "You called me by my name. How could you have known?"

Jesus continued to smile at her but said nothing.

Photini was losing patience, saying, "You didn't answer me. How did you know my name? I've never seen you before, and I have never journeyed outside of Samaria."

Still, Jesus said nothing and continued to look at her with a friendly smile.

"Well, Jesus," she finally said, changing the subject, "why would you come to this well for water, and yet you have no jar and nothing to dip water with. Were you counting on me, to come along and give you a drink?"

"Photini, I was waiting here to talk with you. If you knew the gift of God, and who I am that asks you for a drink, you would ask me and I would give you living water."

"Living water? Are you making light of this situation? Living water, indeed! Where are you getting this water that lives?" she asked. "Are you greater than our father Jacob who gave us this well?"

"I agree, your father, Jacob, was a good man, a godly man. He fathered twelve sons and made excellent choices to follow God, as did most of his sons, especially Joseph."

"You must be a rabbi to have known all that. Jacob is the father of our nation and lived hundreds of years ago."

"That is true," Jesus said with a smile.

She was puzzled by his response. She raised the shadoof again and continued filling her water jar. She then asked, "Well, Jesus, what are you doing here? Are you traveling alone?"

"No, I'm not alone. I am with friends who have gone into the village to get something to eat. We have been in Jerusalem, celebrating Passover, and now are on our way home to Capernaum. I waited here, for you."

"Waited for me? How could you have known I would be here? It was just this morning that I decided to come for water. Yet, you say you waited for me?"

She stopped, remembered something else, then continued, "This water that you say lives, where are you getting it? I would like some of it so that I won't get thirsty and must keep coming here to draw water. What is that water like?"

"We can talk about that," Jesus answered. "I would like to talk with you and your husband. Would you go to your husband and ask that he come back with you?"

"I have no husband," she replied sharply.

"You have answered correctly. You have been with five men in your lifetime, and the one you're living with now is not your husband." Jesus said this with a gentle, compassionate tone.

"Sir, you must be a prophet. If you know that about me, then you know the reasons. The women of my town say the same thing, but they don't care to understand why. They just hold that against me," Photini said as tears came.

"Ah, do you think what you have experienced with your neighbors is like this break we have between our nations?" Jesus asked.

Photini looked away, wiped her tears and took some deep breaths. She thought about what Jesus had asked. "I hadn't thought about that, but, yes, we don't seek answers to our questions. Tell me, Jesus, why do Jews and Samaritans fight so, and not get along? Why is that? Is it the difference in what we believe? I know our ancestors worshipped on this mountain, but you Jews claim that the only place of worship is in Jerusalem. That is certainly one matter that has driven us apart. Which is right? Where should we worship?"

Jesus nodded agreement, then replied, "That is true. But, believe me, Photini, the time is coming when the worship of God will neither be on this mountain nor in Jerusalem, but within the heart. I know that Samaritans have based their worship on what they have learned from the Torah, while Jews worship what they have learned from the prophets and the ancient Scrolls, telling them that salvation is from the Jews. I know that the time is coming, and has already begun, when true believers will worship God in faith, based on spirit and truth. Do you understand?"

Photini had a puzzled look on her face when she answered, "I'm not sure I understand. I know that God is spirit and truth. You say, true believers? Isn't that the same as faith, the same as believing God? And how has it 'already begun'?"

"Yes, you understand that well. You see, God is Spirit, and his true believers will worship God fully in spirit and in truth."

Photini thought about what Jesus was saying, then said, "You say that worship has already begun when believers will worship in the heart. I have heard that the Messiah is coming, and when he comes, things will change. He will explain everything to us, and so we wait for Him".

Jesus looked at her with love and, then declared, "Photini, I am He, the one to whom you are speaking. I am The Messiah."

Photini stared at Jesus in wonder for long moments without saying a word. She became aware that for the first time in her life, she felt no fear, only calmness, and a true sense of who she was.

Then Jesus continued, "You asked me why I would speak to you, a Samaritan woman, and why Jews and Samaritans don't get along? Don't you think it's strange there is a tradition of whole nations of people not talking to one another? Being fearful of one another?"

She looked at him, a thoughtful look on her face, then said, "I agree, it is strange. But it's been going on for hundreds of years. From what I've been told, it has led to violence and people being hurt, even killed. I believe that it is fear that keeps people apart. Fear and misunderstandings, and lack of faith in God."

Jesus thought for a moment, then said, "Yes, you are correct, fear does strange things. What should be done about that? Should we care for one another, even if we live in different regions?"

"Yes, we should," she answered quickly, adding, "we should care for and like one another. But look at me, I'm just an old woman, and no one in this town listens to me!" To which Jesus only smiled.

At that moment, the disciples returned carrying food for their meals and were surprised to see Jesus engaged in conversation with a woman, but they said nothing and waited.

The conversation between the two continued until Photini, leaving her water jar at the well, went back to town to tell people to come and listen to a man who told her everything she ever did. She wondered aloud, as she made her way to town, *He said he was the Messiah. Could he be the Messiah we have talked about? That we have waited for? If he is, what would that mean?*

While the woman was gone, the disciples urged him to eat something, but he declined and proceeded to teach them about the will of God and the role of a disciple.

Later, a group of people from the village followed Photini back to the well. They came tentatively, out of curiosity, but when they heard what Jesus was teaching, they urged him to stay with them. So, Jesus and his disciples remained in the village for two days, teaching and interacting with the people. Because of those days of hearing God's word, and being with Jesus, many Samaritans believed and, over time shared with others what he had taught them.

Chapter 4

AN AMAZING TIME

Now it was morning, two days later, and Photini stood at the edge of town watching Jesus and his followers make their way down the hill in the direction of Capernaum. *What an amazing time this has been*, she thought. *What a blessing it has been to have this man among us. So many in the village embraced him and believed what he was teaching.*

She let all that happened play through her mind. Then she was shaken by something that had happened. Vividly she remembered asking Jesus during that first conversation: *"Where are you getting this water that you say lives. I would like some of it so that I won't get thirsty and have to keep coming here to draw water?"* and Jesus had answered, *"We can talk about that."* But they hadn't. Had they? Then, she had a thought that completely overwhelmed her. One of the town's people had come to her and asked that same question. She had immediately answered, *"Living water is the love that God has for us. It is what Jesus has been teaching. That is what we pass on to others."* The realization that she knew the truth filled her with joy.

The reality of that experience, seeing the love he shared with the people of this village, caused her to have a strong sense of belief that Jesus truly was the Messiah. *He told me he was, now I believe him!* She knew he was her Lord and Savior. *Others need to know this. How will they know this, unless…?*

She wanted to know more about the Messiah, but how could she find out? She knew there was a rabbi in the synagogue at Shechem. She could go there, but would he tell her? Would he even speak to her?

Besides, she thought again, it would not make any difference. She believed in her heart that Jesus was the Messiah! That is all that mattered.

Jesus was now out of sight, yet she continued to look down the road he had taken. She considered the gratitude and love that filled her heart. That had come from Him. That had come from being with Jesus. She was a changed person. *He has given me my life back. No, He has given me a new life.*

Jesus of Nazareth and Capernaum. She knew in her heart that over time He would touch others in His travels, in ways that she could only imagine. She was convinced that the change she saw in so many in her village, was because of His presence, His touch, and His words. That same experience would be repeated and again in other villages throughout His travels. This was an experience that she must tell others about, those who may not have met this Jesus, the Messiah.

Maybe she could introduce them to Him. Could she do that? The thought caused her to smile. Could she travel to other villages and share this story, her story, the story of her people? Yes, she could. She had a purpose, she had value, and she had a reason to smile, to reach out to others, to love them, as the Messiah had said. For the first time in her life, that she could remember, she laughed for joy, even as tears came.

She was certain that his reputation would follow him as he made his way through Galilee and Judea, and probably far beyond. What happened in Sychar and at Jacob's Well, would be among the stories told of Jesus long after he had passed through. She smiled for she knew they would be often repeated, and she would do her part, so that people would know about Jesus, The Messiah.

He was gone now, but she became aware of a new feeling, an awareness, that though Jesus was not here, she still felt His presence, right here, beside her. She no longer felt the old anger that had plagued her for so many years. She knew that He had healed her, as he would heal others. She sensed that in the place of the anger was a lightness, a peaceful confidence deep within. After a while, still smiling, she turned, and started toward town.

Chapter 5

THE MERCHANT

The merchant paced. Although he was in his shop in Tirzah, his mind was a battlefield of conflicting thoughts, tying him in knots. It wasn't just the conflict with his friend Nahman. It wasn't just the stories that he has been hearing about a rabbi. It wasn't just this current struggle about his business and when to begin planning for the next marketing journey. Somehow, he knew he had to resolve each one.

There is no "if," he thought. *I must make another marketing journey, probably in three or four months. There's nothing I can do to get those stories of the rabbi out of my mind. But this conflict with my friend…I have got to fix that! And soon. I know I was wrong, and that probably hurt him. With a little time, we both will calm down, and I'll go to him and hope he will listen. Maybe I can heal this. I must resolve this soon.*

So, he was back to the problem he was having traveling to those markets along the Jordan River. It seemed like for the past several years whenever it was time to begin planning and take that journey, he found himself resisting, not wanting to go. He thought about his father and the family business and how it relied on those sales in those markets along the Jordan.

Shimon had inherited the shop when his father died. He was just seventeen, following the tradition of traveling to markets along the Jordan that had been established by his father. Now, after more than twenty years, what to do? He could end the tradition, a costly decision. The next marketing journey he would be undertaking might be his last, and he would need to make sure that it was profitable. How could he do that? Time would tell.

There they were again, those rabbi stories! Every time he considered ending the market trips, the stories seem to pop up, and he knew why. Regardless of where he travelled, he heard stories of this man. Some called him a carpenter. Some called him rabbi or teacher or even a prophet. Some of the stories were magical: healings, restoring sight, turning water into wine, tales that captivated. It wasn't one story, it was different stories, each one seemed like a fable, just a tale to entertain, and they all did. At each of his stops along the routes he followed, there was a story, to which he would smile and then, discount each, convincing himself it was just a tale. Just a tale, really?

Then, to complicate matters, just a few days after his return from this last journey, three people came into his shop, a man and his wife, along with another woman. They were traveling from Shechem or Sychar and were looking for silk cloth, of a particular color. During the conversation, they told of an amazing experience the people of his village had with a man, a teacher.

The man had pointed to one of the women, and said, "Photini, over there with my wife, spoke to the man first. He was at Jacob's Well when she arrived to get water and asked her for a drink. He was a Jew, maybe a rabbi, a teacher, and he told her he was the Messiah. Can you believe that?"

At that moment the woman stepped over, and said, "I overheard my friend. I am Photini, and that man, Jesus, is more than a teacher. Some call him a carpenter or rabbi, but he told me he was the Messiah, and I believe him. He spent two days in our village talking with all of us about life and loving one another. Before he came, we were divided. So much tension and anger against one another. He changed all of us. I think most of us believe he truly is the Messiah. That was our experience, and we were changed because of it." Having said that, the woman turned and rejoined her friend, examining the silk cloth.

The man had turned to Shimon and explained that the encounter changed Photini from one who was shunned by everyone in the village to a woman responsible for bringing the community together. He called her a leader among the woman and thought that the amazing change in her was all because of this man.

The conversation upset Shimon. It was not what the man said, it was his description of the man called Jesus, which sounded like the carpenter-rabbi of the stories he heard. What he was told, caused him to consider, again, the stories he had heard. What if they weren't tales? Yes, what if…?

The world of Shimon was about to change. What started in little ways over the past year, when he was so engrossed in his shop and preparations for his last market journey, now seemed to occupy his mind. It wasn't any one thing. It wasn't that visit by those people from Sychar and what happened in their town. It wasn't that magical story of turning water into wine, or the healings, even though they were hard to believe, and had come from several different sources. But the fact of the matter was, the stories persisted. They seemed to take on a life of their own. And all of that, taken together, is what really bothered Shimon. It appeared to lend truth and meaning to the question, "What if…?"

But first, he had to make every effort to heal this breach in his friendship with Nahman. *I can't delay any longer. I must go to him, take my chances. We had been close friends for too long and I value his opinion, even when I disagree.*

Chapter 6

RECONCILIATION

Shimon took the long way to Nahman's home, letting his mind sort through what he wanted to say to his friend. *What are the words that could lead to repairing our relationship? Do I say I am sorry? Do I ask for forgiveness? No! Yes! Yes, I do. How? What if he doesn't even let me speak? What if he doesn't even open his door so we can talk? What if…? Whoa, where did that come from?* He heard that often repeated phrase before, in his own mind.

With fearful steps, he reached the front door of Nahman's home. He stood there for long moments before knocking. He waited. One heartbeat, two heartbeats, then, suddenly the door was thrown open, and Nahman was standing there. Without a word, his friend grabbed him in a bear-hug and was saying something that Shimon could not understand. Then he could feel tears on his cheek, his own and his friend's. The hug continued, while they sobbed together.

Finally, Nahman, whipping his face, led him into the gathering room where they sat and looked at one another. Shimon wasn't sure how to begin, but he started, "Nahman…"

"No, Shimon, let me. I must get this out. For long days, I have prayed that we would get together and resolve this. Those three words you gave me so long ago have not left me, but they took on new meaning in my anguish and sorrow at our conflict."

"Three words that I gave you? What are you talking about? What three words?" Shimon asked.

"My friend, you don't remember. I think it was last year, maybe longer. You were just returning from a market journey along the Jordan. I think you had stayed the night in Yardenit. You told me about a conversation you had with a fellow traveler who had been in the synagogue in Capernaum and had listened to a young rabbi who had the most wonderful message. You told me all about that, and we talked about how strange it was that someone would suggest love in the face of all the animosity that we know exists here in Samaria. You told me those three words, 'Love one another' was so hard to understand because of how we feel about the Jews. I think we even chuckled a bit about that, but then we agreed. To love one another would be a good thing.

"I don't know how long ago that was, but I must tell you, Shimon, that phrase, 'love one another,' kept coming back to me, sometimes at the most inopportune times, and it caused me to stop and think. When we both were out of control and I stormed out of your shop, I carried that anger with me until I was almost home, then I stopped, and that phrase came to my mind.

"Shimon, you are my brother, and for all our years together we have loved one another, just as that rabbi had taught. We cannot let this little tangle undo everything we have been given. I ask you to forgive me as I have forgiven you. Let us mend this divide and get on with our lives, together."

"Nahman, I don't know what to say. Once again you have taken my thoughts and words, and spoken to them for both of us. You have said what is on my heart. I want your forgiveness, and, of course, I forgive you. We both spoke out of our pride, not out of our love for one I another. Can we move on? I need you. Your good mind, your common sense, and your friendship."

They continued their conversation well into the afternoon and early evening. They talked only briefly about the incident that brought about the argument and moved on to more important, positive things. In the end, they forged an unofficial partnership, built on trust and respect for one another.

Just before Shimon needed to be on his way home, he introduced some of the ideas that he had about changing his shop and market journeys. It would become a focus of discussions between them in the future. As the two parted, the fierce hug that had started the afternoon continued into their goodbyes. In both their minds, the phrase, "love one another" began to work its magic.

Chapter 7

THE JOURNEY

Circumstance and timing has a way of changing the course of a life. Sometimes in subtle ways, as a small stone can redirect the flow of a mighty stream, altering its course. Sometimes the influence can be startling, forging changes unexpected and long ranging.

A case in point would be Shimon's argument with his friend, Nahman. Their reconciliation had set in motion not only a redefining of their friendship but in the establishment of a partnership in the operation, and character, of the shop, as well as the planning and scheduling of market journeys to the Jordan. As a result of such planning, the marketing journeys would continue, as least for now. The result of those decisions had been surprisingly successful.

The partnership seemed odd to friends. Nahman was quiet, known for his introspection and honesty. Shimon, on the other hand, still had a shifty reputation; in his hometown, he was known as a tough-minded man, one of suspect honesty, a driver of hard bargains, always seeking to profit. On his travels, however, away from Samaria, he was the picture of friendliness, honesty, and generosity. Those customers in the marketplaces saw him as a man that could be trusted, who would never misrepresent the products he sold, and they thought his prices were reasonable. Now, in the shop, the merchant's demeanor had become more welcoming and friendly.

On this day, in the cool of the evening, Shimon was busy with preparations for the marketing journey that would begin early the next morning. In the storage room at the rear of the shop, he had just finished packing the cargo baskets that would be mounted on his mule.

Five days earlier, he and Nahman had made the trip to Caesarea, each leading a mule loaded with cargo baskets. The Bizarre on the wharf was busy when they arrived. Temporary stalls, that had been set up by those importers of goods, were busy throughout the wharf. They focused on the stall carrying special silk cloth from China, another dealing with a variety of handmade goods from India, and one offering exotic spices from the far east. These were the goods that sold well wherever Shimon went.

When they were done, goods that both stocked the shop and those that would make the journey to markets on the Jordan, they were elated with their purchases. As they admired other goods from the far east, Nahman made a strong argument to purchase some of the fine jewelry on display. He thought the beautiful cut stones could be a big seller, especially in the market at Scythopolis. Initially, Shimon resisted, then agreed that it might be a good idea worth trying. Now as he considered the array of goods he would be taking; he could feel that old merchant excitement returning…profits to be made! This will be a good marketing time, he told himself.

Early the next morning, Shimon made his way to the stable and returned leading a mule, outfitted with a cargo harness, and his pride and joy, a coal-black Arabian, named Asam. The baskets, packed with goods for market, were secured on the mule. He then turned his attention to saddling his horse. When all was ready, he mounted and urged Asam forward, leading the mule, turning east, into the rising sun, and the familiar trail that led, eventually, to the Jordan River, eighty kilometers away.

Shimon's mind was fixed on the journey ahead. He knew it would not be easy travelling, rocky and rugged hills and, closer to his destination, an expanse of desert. His first stop would be Afula, a small crossroad village, with a good water source and a decent enough stable, where he would stay the night.

Shimon may have thought that this trip would be routine, like so many he had taken over the years, but he would be mistaken. The merchant was unaware that he was starting his journey on a route that, just days before, the carpenter-rabbi, Jesus of Nazareth, God incarnate, the one some called The Messiah, had followed during the final weeks of a ministry that would change the world. So, the merchant, unaware, traveled on.

Over the years, Shimon's reputation in those markets had grown as a merchant that carried fine silk cloth, as well as exotic spices and perfumes. These were items that sold well and were profitable. This was the same routine he had followed for more than twenty years, and it had become routine. He made friends who looked forward to his arrival. He smiled because he knew there were a few who would try to convince him to return more often.

For this past year, Shimon had been like three different people. To those in Tirzah, who had known him most of his life, he was the model of the people that Jews in Jerusalem despised. Even his long-time colleagues would describe him as less honest, a cheat, and one who could not be trusted. For his part, he had boldly carried the negative Samaritan banner with pride, as if being branded by Jews was a badge of honor.

It was the other Shimon, seen by his customers at the marketplaces along the Jordan River, that attracted customers throughout Syria, Galilee, and Judea to his markets when they knew that he would be there.

But things were changing in his life, in ways over which he had no control. He had never been a religious man, yet, those stories of the carpenter-rabbi he had heard on his journeys, along with that story about the Messiah, all those were on his mind, giving him cause to ponder.

Traveling, regardless how rough the terrain, gave Shimon time to think, and considering all that had happened over the past year or more, he needed that time. All those stories he had heard, stories that he had rejected, that kept coming back to him, and he found his mind playing "What if...s" Yes, what if they weren't just stories? What if he did turn water into wine? What if it was the same man those people from Sychar spoke about, a man who had such an effect on that village? What if…? Indeed!

Shimon just shook his head at all those thoughts. It was just word of mouth, no proof, just stories. Then why did he struggle so? Something was happening to him, he wasn't sure what it was, except some of the thoughts he was having simply overwhelmed him.

Most recently, he wondered about all the hatred, that had persisted for so long. Why was there such continuing distrust and violence between people? Surely, there is a way to set it aside and move on more positively. Where did that come from? Then that phrase came to mind, 'love one another.' How? He knew he had been raised on anger and discrimination. But now, that didn't seem right, and he wondered. *How does one love in the face of hatred and anger?*

The people of Tirzah were the first to notice something was changing with him, even before his own awareness. He seemed to be evolving into a different person, without any effort on his part. His neighbors waited, in vain, for his old anger and dishonesty to emerge. More than all of that, people were drawn to him, to talk to him, in his home and in his shop, just to talk. It was puzzling. He liked it.

He was now skirting the Nablus Mountains, picking his way through rock-strewn hillsides. These were low mountains, but still rugged and nearly tree-less, except for an occasional grove of olive trees, or a solitary, highly prized, Juniper. There on his left was Mount Gerizim, the sacred mountain for the Samaritans with the beautiful temple, a replica of the one in Jerusalem. He simply nodded in that direction and then continued.

The cool of the morning had now given way to the heat of midday, and he knew it would persist until dusk. It would be late afternoon before he would reach the village of Afula. There he would feed and rest his animals in the small stable and spend the night. Afula was the half-way point in his journey to the beautiful city of Scythopolis, on the Jordan River.

Chapter 8
AFULA

It was late in the evening when Shimon arrived in Afula. The stable was clean, as he expected. He selected a stall where he could store his goods and stable his animals. After brushing and feeding the animals, he placed his saddle near the stall entrance and prepared a place where he could spend the night, resting and watching over his property. From a saddle bag, he took out food for his evening meal, a skin of water, and settled himself for the night.

There were other travelers, staying in the stable, and he listened to their conversations. It was here, on his last journey, that he heard some of those tales of a man, they called a carpenter or prophet. Now, one man was telling a story he had first heard in Caesarea, about a man turning water into wine. Again, Shimon smiled to himself, thinking "Oh, to be able to do that. I would be a wealthy man". But he said nothing.

The stable owner came by, checking on those staying. When he heard the others sharing stories, he spoke up, "Let me tell you something that is both interesting and true. This is not a tale, for I saw this with my own eyes, right here, just four or five days ago. There was a man, he could have been a rabbi, but he didn't look like one, who passed through my little village, traveling with some of his followers. I think they were heading in the direction of Capernaum.

"Now, in this village of mine, we get our share of sick people passing through, including lepers, you know, those who smell bad and whose skin is rotting. We don't want them anywhere near our town. These are people who, if you even touch them, you will get their illness all over your skin, and you will die. Just like that.

"Well, just a few days ago, there was a group of these lepers staying far off, just over there, outside the village limits, within that circle of stones," pointing. "This stranger, this rabbi, came by late in the morning, with some friends. The lepers raised their voices, calling out to him saying 'Master, have mercy on us!' I thought they would ask to be healed, but that is not what they said. Can you imagine? Why were they asking him for mercy? I don't know. He walked among them, and talked to them for a while, encouraged them, and even prayed with them. Then he told them to go and talk to a holy person, and, if they believed, they would be healed. That is what he said. 'If you believe you would be healed.' Can you imagine? I was right here, cleaning these stables and I could hear every word.

"Those people, those lepers, got all excited, they gathered what they owned, and left. I suppose they went looking for a holy man. They must have found something, because one of them came back, one that had lived in this town, shouting praises that he, and the others, had been healed! He sought out the rabbi, for he wanted to praise him for the mercy and his healing. Of course the rabbi had already gone on his way.

"I know, I know this is hard to believe. How do I know he was healed? Well, I told you that the man lived here, before he got sick, and had to leave our community. But now that he was healed, he wanted to return. Before the town would allow that, he had to prove that he was no longer ill. The town leaders couldn't believe he had been healed, but after he showed them that he had no sign of this sickness, his skin was cleared of any infection, they were astounded! He was healed! He had been a leper, and very sick, but now he was healed!

"If you doubt what I have said, you could ask him yourself. Every morning, early, he is in the town square, singing morning praises to God and dancing around the square, like a crazy, happy man. Was he healed, by that man, that rabbi? I don't know. Were the others healed? I don't know that either. I do not know how to explain what happened, except that I believe the stranger, the rabbi, made all the difference. I tell you, I saw most of this, so I know it is not just a tale."

One of the travelers scoffed, "How do you know they were even sick in the first place?"

"Have you ever seen a leper? Have you ever smelled a leper? Well, I have, lots of them, and these people were lepers. As I said that one lives here. I knew him before he got sick, and I watched his sickness spread until he had to be ordered out of the town, nearly dead. It was a sad time for his family and his friends. Now he has returned, and he is one of us again."

Another, asked, "Maybe, on their way to the priest or a holy one, they were healed some other way, or by another source?"

The stableman had no answer, and simply said, "I don't know. What I do know is, they were lepers, and then one returned, and he was healed, and he told us that the others were as well. That is all I know. Go talk to him in the morning, down in the square."

The merchant thought about what he had heard, and just smiled, shook his head, and settled himself near his animals. *A group of lepers healed*, he thought. *Impossible!* That is another strange story. He did like the one about a carpenter who turned water into wine. That story always made him laugh. Again, he thought, *I could make a wonderful profit if I could learn that trick. Healing of lepers, water into wine, interesting stories, but just that, stories.*

Then another thought that caused him to wonder anew. *The stableman said the man that healed the lepers had been here, in Afula, just days before. Why? Maybe heading toward the Jordan River? This same route I am on. What if...* He shook his head, trying to dismiss a disturbing thought.

He tried to think where these stories came from. Yes, he heard some on his travels, like this one about the lepers. He heard several in his own shop from pilgrims going to Mount Gerizim to worship, or simply travelers through Samaria. Regardless of the story, they were nothing more than tales, interesting and entertaining. He smiled and closed his eyes. Yet, before he dozed off, that one little, nuisance phrase came back into his mind, what if…? Yes, what if there was some truth? With that thought, he closed his eyes and slept.

It was still dark, just before dawn, when Shimon awoke, repacked his saddle bags, and prepared for the next part of his journey, the hard part across the last of the Nablus Mountains, then through the desert to the Jordan River. He cinched his cargo harness on his mule, loaded the baskets of his goods, and saddled his horse. It was still dark when he quietly led them from the stable, down the road, across the square to the town well. He filled his jars with fresh water and was ready to travel.

He was preparing to mount his horse when he heard singing. He looked around the square. There, on the far side of the square, in the gathering morning light, he could just make out a man, dancing and singing something that could only be described as a truly joyful song of praise. The words of the sable-man came back to him, *"He is usually in the town square, early in the morning. He will be the one who is singing praises."*

Shimon watched, mesmerized, as he could now see the man clearly, dancing around in celebration. *Yes*, thought Shimon, *that is probably the man he was talking about, but was he a leper who might have been healed by the rabbi-carpenter? I can't believe that. It just couldn't be! There is no cure for leprosy. An interesting story? Yes. A healing? No! That man there…a coincidence? Should he speak to him? No. It's just a story, like what children tell one another, and he would be looked upon as crazy for asking such a question. Besides, he had a long journey ahead of him.*

With that, he mounted his horse, and quietly left the square. It would be much later when Shimon would have cause to regret this decision. Still, as he left the small town of Afula, his mind was filled with stories, tales, and that bothersome phrase that kept coming to mind: What if these stories were not stories? What if…?

Chapter 9
A GIRL ALONE

Eight years earlier, on dusty side streets and marketplaces of Jerusalem, a little girl begged to survive. She was just a waif, eleven years old, all skin and bones, and all alone. Her name was Naomi, and there was no one to take care of her, both parents were gone. Her home, if you could call it that, was a tiny shack, just inside the southern gate, the Dung Gate, where the city dumped all the garbage, trash, and, yes, manure. The smell from the trash heap was constant, often keeping her from sleep and the loneliness stirred up sadness in the heart of the child, causing her to cry.

Her life had changed, in fits and starts, beginning, when Roman soldiers came and took her father into the army, assigning him to a far-off post. Neither she, nor her mother, would see him again. She was just barely six years old. She had few memories of him, and even now, she had a hard time remembering his face, which made her sad and deepened her loneliness.

Then, four years after her father was taken away, her mother, beloved by the women of her community, had become ill, and the sickness progressed to the point where she had been forced to live outside of the city. Leprosy, they told the child, the dreaded disease of uncleanness. Even to their closest friends she was an untouchable, forced to live alone, without her daughter. Friends took Naomi in and tried to make her a member of their family, but after a few weeks, she ran away, an unsuccessful attempt to find her mother. Then it happened again, and again. Finally, they let her run.

Now, at age eleven, Naomi had not seen her mother for a year, and, down deep, she knew she would never be held in those loving arms. The fact that she was by herself, without family or friends, saddened her deeply, and fed her anger. She began to think of herself, not as Naomi but as "the bitter one," and, it was then that she started calling herself Mara, the Hebrew word for bitter. She was bitter, and it reflected on her face, and she began to develop a cautious and distrusting nature. Seemingly, no one would help her, no one would take care of her, and she roamed the dangerous city, begging for food, just another stray dog.

It was a rabbi who noticed her hanging around the temple courtyard and felt pity. He tried to talk to her, but she would just scamper away. He began to watch for her, on and around the Temple Mount; timid, cautious, relying on the good graces of others, from a distance. One night he heard her in one of the many baptism pools that surrounded the temple, cooling off from the heat of the day. After that, nearly every evening, he would set food out for her, by the pools, near the statue of Moses in the courtyard, and noted that in the morning it would be gone. He inquired to various communities as to her family, but no one seemed to remember who the parents were, or what had happened to them.

Over time, a degree of trust formed between the girl and the rabbi, and he was able to talk with her, from a distance. He now knew that her mother had been sent to the restricted leper colony, but it was uncertain if she was still alive. No one had knowledge of her father. Beyond that, nothing more.

Then, one day, following morning prayers, an elderly lady saw the girl in the courtyard and approached the rabbi, telling him, what he already knew, that she knew the child and thought that her mother, resided in the leper colony, if she was still alive. She went on to say that she believed the mother had a brother living outside Jerusalem, maybe in a nearby village, she didn't know anything else.

Another woman, standing nearby and overhearing the conversation, spoke up and agreed that there was a brother, and she thought he ran an inn, just north of Jerusalem. She seemed to recall that his name was Aaron, or something like that, but she wasn't certain. She did think that the inn was on or near the road to Jericho, just beyond the Mount of Olives.

And, so it was, that the rabbi, finally verified what he had been told, and, with some effort, convinced the girl to go with him to meet her uncle, who was an innkeeper, and whose name turned out to be Abbas. The meeting was awkward. There was resistance from both the girl and her uncle. However, after some discussion, both reluctantly agreed to give it some time. So, now, at age twelve, Naomi, calling herself Mara, was given a safe and warm place to stay, clean clothes, regular food, and assigned tasks that she was expected to do at the Inn on Jericho Road.

Chapter 10

SCHOOLING MARA

Abbas was a gruff Jew, a businessman who ran the Inn with an uncompromising hand. He had a firm policy and would only accept Jews in his establishment. As for this niece, he did not like being forced to take in this daughter of his sister. He looked upon the responsibility as an unwelcome burden and, immediately, treated her as an employee, assigning her to a full array of cleaning tasks throughout the Inn.

Mara, on the other hand, gladly welcomed the work. She did not need to beg. She had a safe, sweet-smelling place to stay, regular food, a place to bath, and a warm place to sleep, which was immediately appealing to the young girl. It did not take long for her to cease being a little girl, as she learned her place and duties well, taking responsibility seriously. In time, she became a nearly invisible, hard-working member of the Inn's service staff. Through other workers and her uncle, she learned well the requirements of the inn, even beyond her assigned duties.

Over time, the Innkeeper began to see her as a young woman who was quickly becoming a valued member of his staff and a relative. When she had been there a year, in difference to his Jewish roots, Abbas took Mara into Jerusalem and to the temple to meet with a teacher of the Law, for instruction and the ceremony of dedication. The experience touched the young girl deeply, causing her to realize that, finally, she was part of a real family.

When Mara was fourteen, Abbas allowed her to accompany him to Bethany to buy supplies. In the market, she happened to meet a woman, named Martha, whom she liked immediately. The friendly conversation continued while Abbas made the purchases they needed.

As they were getting ready to leave, to return to the Inn, Martha approached Abbas, and offered to teach Mara to read and give her instruction with numbers. Abbas' immediate answer was "No. Mara has too much to do at the Inn and for her to travel to Bethany alone was out of the question. The matter is settled."

"But, uncle," Mara said, "Think about it. I could be of more help to you at the Inn if I knew numbers."

"I said, no!"

Martha spoke up, "Innkeeper, maybe there is another solution. My sister, Mary, and I could travel to the inn together, and we could at least get started, giving Mara enough, so that she could work on your own. I sense that she is a bright, young lady. Maybe our brother could come with us, for safety."

Abbas thought about the offer. He was never good at numbers, and maybe there was value in this for him, and for the inn. Having Mara able to read, could be helpful, too. So, reluctantly, he granted his permission, and the arrangement was set.

A few weeks later, Mary and Martha, accompanied by their brother, Lazarus, arrived at the Inn, late in the morning, and spent most of the day instructing Mara in reading and numbers. The two sisters realized the girl was an able student, who quickly, and excitedly, learned the basics of reading and the logic of numbers. The sisters found Mara to be smart and clever, and wholly engaged in the schooling process. But there was more, they discovered in her a lively sense of humor and a capacity for listening which was a pleasant surprise.

So, it was, after only two such visits, weeks apart, that the girl had a firm grasp on what the sisters could teach her. She realized that what she was learning could be applied directly to the operation of the inn. Over time, she excitedly explained to Abbas, what she had learned, especially her skills with numbers, and how that could be turned into great value, both to Mara and to the inn. She convinced him that she added value to the operation of the inn, and her duties were expanded accordingly.

Meanwhile, throughout the two visits, Lazarus, and Abbas, found common interests and spent some time walking around the inn, discussing ways to improve the hostel. They seemed to enjoy each other's company, and sat outside for extended periods, deep in animated conversation, going over plans for expansion of the inn and how the work could be accomplished without interrupting present operations.

The hard work of the inn shaped the girl into a young woman whose attractiveness, sense of humor and quiet efficiency, shown through, reshaping her outlook. It was her influence that seemed to enhance the welcoming environment of the inn. It became clear that deep within her heart lay the qualities that had marked her mother as a compassionate and caring person.

As the years passed, Mara became an important part of the management of the inn, and Abbas, more inclined toward hosting and socializing with guests, gradually, came to rely on her sharp, serious mind, and good judgment. In reality, the two were good partners and the inn flourished, with a reputation as a welcoming waystation on the rugged and dangerous road that lead, north, down to Jericho.

Chapter 11

SCYTHOPOLIS

The sun was just cresting the eastern horizon, nearly blinding Shimon as he rode out of Afula, and headed into the mountains that stood between him and the desert. This part of his journey would be exhausting, through the last of the rugged hills and ravines of the Nablus Mountains, then the long journey through the desert. The brightness of the sun promised another hot day, before his arrival at the grand city of Scythopolis, on the Jordan River.

His travel always gave him time to think, even times when he would talk to his horse, like a crazy man! He thought again of those stories he had been hearing for months and his mind played tricks. *What if...* he thought. *What if those stories were all true?* He had to smile at the thought. A healer of lepers and a winemaker! What a combination. There had been other stories, some even more magical, that he had heard, and he supposed he would hear more as he continued to travel. Then a ridiculous thought came to mind, and he laughed out loud, startling his horse. *What if this carpenter, this rabbi could fly? Or perhaps take a walk across the Sea of Galilee. Imagine? That would be something to see. Maybe that would convince him that the stories were real.* He continued to chuckle as he rode on.

The way was rugged through the mountains, slow going as he picked his way through, avoiding the Sabar cactus with its long thorns, and through difficult passes. Occasionally, being rewarded by a Jaffa orange tree with fruit there for the picking. Frequently he would stop, check the straps holding his precious cargo baskets in place, give his animals rest and water. He would treat himself to a bit of fruit, would have some water, then they were on their way. Occasionally he would pause to marvel at the stark beauty of the panorama of distant mountains and valleys.

He thought again of those stories, a mystery man who could do marvelous tricks. *Why was each story credited to a rabbi or a carpenter? I mean, after all, isn't there a difference between what they wear? Don't you think you would know if you were meeting a rabbi? I think I could tell if the man was a common worker, just from the tunic he was wearing. Besides, a carpenter turning water into wine! I would like to taste that wine,* and the thought brought a smile. *And that story about the lepers. Maybe it was the carpenter who rebuilt the lepers,* to which he had to laugh, again. Then, a sobering thought: *He should have spoken to that man in the square back in Afula. One or two questions would have proved that it was just a story.*

He traveled on, now focused on Scythopolis and the marketplace. This city was his favorite destination. It was a beautiful place and the market there had always been profitable. Customers came from great distances because they liked the goods offered, and because Shimon had the reputation of carrying the highly prized, and rare, purple silk cloth.

Finally, late in the day, he rode to the top of a rise, and paused, taking in the beautiful view. There, below him, lay the city with the Jordan River just beyond. He had always marveled at this point in his journeys, because the city was the most beautiful place he had ever been to. Paved streets, busy with people coming and going. Ornate buildings, walkways of marble and a vast marketplace, always a welcome sight. Whenever he was in this city, the sight of all this beauty and luxury, encouraged him, and he stayed in the best inn, dined on the finest, exotic dishes, and treated himself to the very best of whatever was available. Expensive? Yes. Worth it? Yes.

His first stop was the city stable, adjacent to the marketplace, there he arranged feed and water for his animals, and acquired a place to secure his goods for the night. As he dismounted, it felt so good to be off his horse and stretching. He was looking forward to a walk around to admire all that the city had to offer.

Later his stroll brought him to the Inn, a beautiful building, with ornate arches, large windows, polished stone, and marble everywhere. He arranged for a room and was told the evening meal was being served. He realized that he was hungry and congratulated himself on his perfect timing. In time he was seated at a table by one of the windows. All the walls of the dining room were adorned with artistic tapestries, each telling a story of life along the Jordan River. There were representations of caravans of camels entering the city, boats along the Jordan approaching an ornate wharf, busy streets, flags, and banners everywhere, and happy people.

One glance at the menu and it didn't take him long to realize how hungry he was. The special for the evening was lamb brisket. *What, good fortune*, he thought. He selected a nice collection of olives, figs and dates, along with fresh baked bread, and, of course, the lamb. "Now, bring on the wine," he said to the waiter, with a smile.

As he sat waiting for his order, he listened to all the talk around him. He became aware that he was hearing some of the same stories, about this rabbi-carpenter. But then his attention became focused on a group of men sitting at a table near him. One man was telling about an experience he had recently in Tiberius. The Roman Captain of the guard at the Synagogue approached the rabbi and begged him to come home and help his twelve-year-old daughter who was ill until death. By the time, they got to the captain's home the little girl had died. Apparently, the rabbi told the captain to not be afraid but to believe in him. Shortly after that, he took the girl by the hand and she came alive and he told her to get up and asked her mother to give her something to eat. The speaker then said, "I know this happened because I was there. I couldn't believe what was happening."

Shimon wondered how could that possibly be true? Dead, and now raised to life! Yet some believed it. He couldn't help but wonder if they were talking about the same man that supposedly, healed lepers?

Shimon continued to listen, and other men shared what they had heard and seen during their time in Tiberius and other parts of northern Galilee. They referred to a man, again a rabbi-carpenter, who lived in the area around Capernaum. They, too, had heard some of the same tales he had heard, but there were also others. It seems this man had powers to heal the sick and cause the lame to walk. One of the men said he had heard him speak, and he had a wonderful message and told interesting stories, about living in peace.

The conversations continued throughout the meal, sharing stories heard, but some of them expressed doubt and joked about who this man could be. No one seemed to give full credence to some of what they had heard. Yet, to Shimon, their conversation added to his growing wonder—was there truth in these stories?

Chapter 12

STORIES TOLD

Shimon listened to the storytelling around him as he finished his meal. Then, he spoke up and told them about his experience in Afula, and the healing of the lepers. Several of the men laughed and thought the story ridiculous. One man asked, "Why didn't you speak to the healed one, you know, just to be certain it was just a story?" Shimon had no answer to that, and again he felt regret.

But then, toward the end of the meal, an older man, seated at a table nearby, spoke up: "Forgive me for listening to your conversations, but I must tell you about my experience. This was more than four months ago, I was traveling from Pella, east of the Jordan, through cities of the Decapolis, to Bethsaida, where I was staying. One afternoon I saw this man, I suppose the same one you refer to as a rabbi. He had a kind face. He didn't look like a carpenter, he was just an ordinary man, except for his hands. He had the hands of one who worked with wood and stone. He wasn't dressed like a rabbi, but his voice, so warm and inviting, and what he was teaching was like a learned one.

"I was curious. I had heard some of these same stories about him that you were telling, it seemed everywhere I traveled. So, when I had the opportunity, I followed a large crowd, that gathered on a hillside to listen to him. I ended up staying all afternoon and, I have to say he was a wonderful teacher, sharing inspirational thoughts and ideas, some in stories that had meaning. Frankly, I was taken by him. He spoke of God, as if God was his loving father, if you can imagine that. And he told of peace, but it was more than that. He related to us as if we were old friends, as if he loved us, truly loved us. It was an amazing experience." The man paused, as if he was trying to decide what to say next."

All attention was now focused on the man, waiting to hear what more he had to share.

The man looked around the room, seemed to wipe tears from his cheeks, then he continued, "Late that afternoon, we had been there all day, he did something that I will never forget. Never!" At that, the man seemed to choke back a sob, he shook his head, and then turned away from the men, lost in his own recollections. After a pause, he simply resumed eating.

The men looked at one another, until one of them said: "My friend, we are sorry to interrupt your meal, but, please, could you finish what you were saying? What happened? What did the man do that you will never forget? It seems that it must have been something that touched you, deeply. It must have been important. Can you share that with us?"

The man turned to him, and then looked at each of the others, in turn. For a long moment he said nothing, then he took a sip from his cup, set it down, then began: "All right, I'll tell you exactly what I experienced. This is not a story I'm telling you, not some made-up fable. You must understand, I was there in that crowd, on that hillside. I do not lie! I watched everything that was happening and, even now, I find it hard to believe what I saw, and what I experienced.

"I told you there was a large crowd. There were thousands on that hillside, men, women, and children. Do you understand? Thousands. Many had been there for two days."

The man paused. Again, he had tears in his eyes, as he recalled that moment. There was silence throughout the dining room. All were paying attention to what the man was saying.

Wiping his face with a cloth, the man composed himself, and then continued: "I don't know how to say this so that you would understand what happened." Long pause, deep breath, then he blurted out. "He fed us! Do you understand, what I just said? He fed us! I ate a meal of bread and fish that he provided right there on the hillside. I am telling you that he fed thousands and thousands of people. He fed us! Do you hear me? Do you understand the impossibility of what I am saying? Of what I experienced?" The man paused, wiped his eyes again.

Then he continued, "From where I was sitting on the hillside, I saw this man, this rabbi, you call him, take a small loaf of bread and a piece of fish, he lifted them high above his head, blessed them, then broke pieces into a basket. Then his followers started to pass out baskets, each one loaded with fresh food. It was an amazing thing, an impossible thing. To my mind, it was a miracle."

At the mention of a miracle, those in the dining room started talking to one another. The man raised his voice and said, "Listen to me!" The room quieted, and he continued: "I told you I wasn't sure what I was seeing, but that's not true. What I saw and what I experienced, happened. I ate the food! I had my fill! There was more left over. Baskets of it. It was real, and yet, there was something else." And tears began to fall again.

"What?" one man asked. "Something else? Tell us. Don't stop. What else happened?"

"No, go back to your meals," he said as he wiped his eyes, and took a deep breath, and considered if he should say more. After a long pause, he continued: "It wasn't what happened there, as powerful as that was. It's what has happened to me, since. I came away shaken and I still can't get that whole scene out of my mind. It has been months, but I can't forget that experience. What that man had said, what he told all of us, the man that you call a rabbi, is…I don't know…I think he is more than a prophet. He is not an ordinary man; I can tell you that. He is a Holy man. He is a man of God. This experience has changed me. I tell you it has changed me. Since that day, wherever I have traveled, I have shared my experience, and I have been a different person."

With that, the man stood, looked at all those who had been listening, then simply turned, and walked out of the dining room, shaking his head, and wiping his tears. The room was deadly quiet for long moments, each man thinking about all that had been said.

Chapter 13
UNTIL I SEE PROOF

The dining room was silent, processing what they had heard, until Shimon spoke up. "What do you think about that? That was quite a story. Thousands fed by this carpenter, this rabbi. Did you believe him?"

One of the men commented, "I do. I had heard about the feeding of that crowd before. I came from the north, from Caesarea Philippi, and stopped in Bethsaida for supplies. That is when I heard about it from several people on my travels. People who were there. Let me tell you, they had the same reaction. I, too, thought it was just a story, but they were convincing.

"Now, we all heard the same thing, what we heard here was from one who was there. Do I doubt that he was there? No. Do I think this was just another story? No. That man was caught up in something larger than himself. Do I believe him? Yes, I do. I don't know what it means, but I believe that man, that man of God, whatever you want to call him, did what they say.

"Something else. He is not another rabbi, and he certainly is not a carpenter. I was not on the hillside, I did not listen to this holy man, nor did I eat of his bread and wine. But I believe from all that was said that this Jesus is a holy man, a man of God. If I believe that, then I believe what he teaches. If I believe what he teaches, then I believe he fed thousands from nothing. That is a miracle. Getting me to believe in God, that is another miracle. And I believe!"

There was nervous laughter and smiles throughout the dining room.

"Well, you can believe what you wish. As for me? I not so sure," Shimon said. "I've heard many stories, many fables, but are any of them true? We don't really know. This one, feeding a crowd. Really? Yes, he seemed greatly affected by the experience, but I am still doubtful. If I believed this one, then what about all these other stories? Then, which one will I accept next?" With that, Shimon returned to his food.

Another man spoke directly to Shimon. "Sir, did you see that man? Did you hear him? Those were real tears of a man who had experienced something powerful. I don't think that was an act, nor do I think it was a tale. I think that man was there and witnessed exactly what he told us. I agree, what he described is a miracle, by that carpenter, or rabbi, or whoever he is. But nevertheless, something truly amazing happened."

Still another man said, "For years I was a skeptic, like our friend here," pointing to Shimon. "But think about this. What about all those stories we were talking about? We don't know if they are true. But we keep hearing them repeated wherever we go. We heard some of these stories from two who were followers of this man, this carpenter; those who had witnessed this man's amazing ministry. They spoke of calming a storm out on the Sea, and healings they had seen with their own eyes, including a crippled man restored. It is hard not to believe these men, these disciples.

"You asked if these stories were true? I don't know. We only know that we heard so many throughout our travels from Capernaum and Tiberius, from people who believed them, and what they described was convincing. I have to say, I am inclined to believe that whoever did some of these things, is special. Maybe he is, as that man told us, a man of God."

Shimon stood, shaking his head. "Again, I say, I'm not convinced. Until I see proof, those are no more than stories. I told you about my experience in that town of Afula. The story about a stranger who healed a group of lepers. Think about that. Did it happen? I didn't see it. Do I take the word of a stableman or was he just entertaining us?"

"But, why didn't you follow through and speak to the healed man? Were you afraid that a healing had actually occurred, and this carpenter was the reason?" one man challenged.

"Believe me, I wish I had. Maybe, I was thinking about what I had heard about him in Caesarea, about a man turning water into wine. I am still skeptical. These stories are hard to believe. They defy common sense. I'm not sure what I would've found out if I had talked to that man in Afula, but it's too late now."

Another of the men said, "Wait a minute. I heard about that, the turning water into wine. It was at a wedding in Cana, and the friend who told me about it was there, in attendance. When he first told me, I, too, thought it was a story, but my friend is a rabbi, and he does not tell tales. Did it happen? My friend said it did. Did I see it with my own eyes? No, but my friend did, and had some of the wine. Do I believe my friend? Yes, I do."

They nodded, then another spoke up saying that there was something about all the stories they had heard that caused them to want to share them with others. Turning to Shimon, he said, "Maybe the carpenter, or rabbi or the stranger were the same person, and he was a healer, or, perhaps, just an ordinary man, a really good storyteller, but maybe not. If the stories are all true, think what that could mean.

"Feeding a crowd? Well, that one is hard to believe, but that man from Pella was really shaken. His tears were real, and it was obvious that something had touched him. Yes, I guess I do believe that one. Even though the man was called a carpenter, and apparently looked like one, I believe the stories are really about a rabbi, a 'Man of God'".

Shimon persisted, "I don't even want to think about that. Each one of us must make that decision to believe or not for himself. If you believe the stories you have heard, then he must be a Holy Man or a magician. If you are doubtful, like me...well.

"But here's the thing, did you actually see any of these healings? Did you witness magical happenings? Did any of you see that "rabbi" feeding a crowd? Do we simply believe the storyteller? As for me, unless I see it with my own eyes, those things you have called a miracle, I just won't believe any of it."

The others just looked at him and shook their heads.

Shimon finished his meal in silence. He continued to have doubts about all these stories, thinking they were just made-up fairy tales, told to entertain. A healer? A man of God? Indeed! What do these men know, anyway? They weren't there! And neither was I!

He walked from the dining hall, through town, to the marketplace where he arranged for a venue to set up his goods for the next morning. He looked around the marketplace. It was a beautiful, expansive place, and he felt a familiar glow, thinking about the profits he had made here in the past.

As he made his way back to the Inn, he thought again about the man from Pella and what he had said about that teacher, that carpenter. *What if it were true? No. Get that out of your mind*, he told himself. *Feeding a crowd from what? Nothing, nothing at all. I couldn't believe something like that unless I saw it with my very own eyes and ate some of that food. Phooey! They are all just made-up stories, interesting, but still tales.*

The next morning, true to his expectations, there were customers waiting when he opened his stall for business, showcasing a beautiful array of goods. Throughout the day people would come and go, some making purchases, while others just wanted to talk to Shimon, to hear of his 'travel', stories he invented which seemed to engage customers and help with sales. With a smile he thought, my stories are tales for sales. Maybe that was what all these carpenter fables were about – tales for sales. But what were those stories selling? Maybe selling isn't the right word. Maybe the question is, what are we to believe? If we believe the stories, what is the purpose?

By late afternoon, with few buyers still around and his store of quality goods somewhat diminished, he closed his stall. It had been a good day. He repacked his goods, secured them, then headed back to the Inn for dinner and a good night's rest. In the morning, he would travel to the market town of Gadara, a day's journey along the Jordan

River, then east up the Jabbok a short distance. There he hoped to sell all his remaining goods, and even his mule, before returning home.

Chapter 14
CONFLICT BREWING

Jerusalem, several months earlier. It was late afternoon when a tall man, dressed in clerical robes, left the temple in Jerusalem, heading for his home, just beyond the Temple Mount. His name was Yosef, he was a Sadducee, who, just last year, had been elected to the Sanhedrim. At thirty-five, he was the youngest member of that cabinet. He was a proud man.

But, on this day, he was not a happy man. The events of Passover Week had really gotten to him and caused him to wonder about this conflict he was having between Mosaic law, ingrained in him by his Pharisee father, and throughout his rabbinical training, and some of the stories he had been hearing. His whole life had been grafted into The Law, so, now, why this conflict? Why this doubt?

It was here, in the Sanhedrin that the conflict raised its ugly head. The dispute centered around the influence that a radical rabbi from Galilee seemed to be having on a small segment of the Jewish population, an influence that seemed to directly contradict some specifics of Mosaic Law, as interpreted by both Pharisee and Sadducee.

Yosef was often outspoken and bold, expressing his opinions, sometimes to the displeasure of others. So, as he listened to the discussion, he wondered why there was so much emotion expressed. What little he knew about that rabbi and what he had been teaching, and his popularity, he wondered, often aloud so all could hear, why it seemed to pose such a threat to established and long-standing Mosaic law in the eyes of the Pharisees.

The heated discussion continued until Gamaliel rose and stood before the Sanhedrin. He was the most respected member of that body, and his quiet presence carried a strong influence on all. The old teacher had always called for "reasonable dialogue" and calmness. Now, with a wry smile, he addressed the gathering: "Fellow members of the Sanhedrin, let us consider that it has been a year or two since our 'Brother Moses' entrusted us with the Sacred Scrolls, and, their meaning, and behold, they have survived!" This caused something unusual and rare to happen, laughter within the Holy Temple! Heat drained from the arguments, and calm discussion returned, at least for a time.

Gamaliel continued, "What is the real threat? Is our pride getting in the way? Can this carpenter from Galilee, this 'radical rabbi' as you call him, cause us to turn away from the Law as we know it? As our young colleague, Yosef, has often expressed, where is the conflict, where is the threat?"

"But, Teacher," one of the elder Sadducees argued, "while I have not listened to this mad rabbi, I have heard it said that much of what he preaches appears contrary to our beliefs. If what he is teaching is right in the eyes of the Lord, then most of what we have lived and taught is wrong. More and more of the people are following him, and that is cause for grave concern."

"Ah, my brother, you make a good point," the old rabbi said. "Indeed, what does this 'mad rabbi', as you call him, teach?"

Just then, Nicodemus, a Pharisee of note, rose and stood beside Gamaliel. "Let me add another perspective to this discussion. Most of you do not know this but, not that long ago, I spoke to this rabbi, this Jesus of Nazareth, and asked him questions about what he was teaching. I listened carefully to what he had to say. He spoke of being born a second time. Can you imagine? I questioned him on that point, and it seemed magical, difficult to understand, and contrary to convention. As we parted, I told him that in my reasoned judgment, his teachings seemed unorthodox, too simplistic, or mysterious to truly be followed.

"Fellow members of the Sanhedrin, in our conversation, I have heard nothing that would change my mind, nor am I persuaded that his teaching is a threat. I am surprised, however, on two points. First, considering what I heard from him, how do ordinary men understand what he teaches? I don't believe they do. My second point is this, I am surprised at his current popularity among the people. Again, in my reasoned judgment, this is a temporary situation, and will not long endure. I repeat, I found little that should threaten us." Nicodemus then nodded and returned to his place at the table.

Gamaliel remained standing and listened to what was being said, as discussion resumed. Then he raised his hand for silence. "Thank you, Brother Nicodemus, for that important perspective on this rabbi from Galilee. I believe you are the only one among our group that has listened carefully to what this Jesus has to say. Perhaps, it would be good if other members would find time to listen to his teaching and determine if his popularity is, as Nicodemus reported, temporary and will not last long, or if his teaching does pose what some consider "a threat." May I suggest that one or two of us, spend some time listening to this teacher and then present your first-hand witness to this august body. At that point, we could make some kind of reasoned declaration."

This suggestion caused a wave of mumbling decent throughout the Sanhedrin, many shaking their heads. Finally, one expressed the opinion that if it became known that the Sanhedrin was listening to this man, it could add credence to what he was teaching and that could drive many into his blasphemous lies.

Gamaliel listened quietly, then, again, raised his hands for silence, "If you fear or simply would prefer not to seek out this rabbi and listen to him as a group, might I suggest that one of us, quietly observe him. Maybe young Yosef, here, would be a good and honest representative of this body. His singular presence among the crowd listening to this rabbi, would not cause concern. Besides, he is strong, and we have come to know him, as one with a good mind, who has shown good judgement. If he agrees, and has our support, I suggest that we await a time when he has something to report before we resume our discussion."

The Sanhedrin considered this for a time, then unanimously agreed for Yosef, to be their representative, and to seek out this radical rabbi when he is in the area and hear what he has to teach. With that, the High Priest, Ananus, adjourned the meeting until the appointed next gathering when Yosef would, possibly, have something to report.

And, so, Yosef was not happy as he left the Temple. He was conflicted. He had pride that the governing body had entrusted him with this important task. But this very task played into his own conflict, unresolved, and a source of discomfort for him. He must discuss this with his wife, Deborah, he thought. Then, with a sigh, he walked on toward his home, shaking his head.

Chapter 15

OLD-SCHOOL VS.??

Yosef continued toward home, the matter, unsettled. He did not want this assignment, yet, strangely, he had felt a sense of pride that he had been recognized as worthy. He had no interest in listening to this carpenter, the so-called rabbi, thinking that whatever camel dung he is spouting, would have no value to him or to the Sanhedrin, and it would not help him resolve this new conflict he seemed to have. He would listen to the man, make his report, and make his old teacher proud.

In many ways, he considered himself aligned with old school Sadducees, and was comfortable with their interpretation of the sacred scrolls. Still, he had some thoughts that had plagued him for years in his understanding of Mosaic law. He had heard the talk about some of the carpenter's teachings, which caused him to wonder where was the conflict, where was the threat? Maybe it was the growing number of followers that bothered them. Could it be that superficial?

He remembered one confrontation he was told about, when the rabbi was challenged for not washing his hands before eating, as was prescribed by Mosaic law. Yosef thought both the challenge and the law were questionable, and maybe unnecessary. It was a little thing, but still.

Later that night, after the children were put to bed, he un-burdened himself of the conflict that still troubled him. Deborah was a good and strong Jewish wife. She clearly recognized that he was the head of household, but there were times when her strong will and reasoning pushed for other changes. He spoke to her about some of the practices of the Sadducee, that seemed to him to be less than religious, more political, and not in keeping with Mosaic Law. He also wondered about the close relationship which the Sadducee leadership seemed to have with Rome, and that made him uncomfortable.

Deborah listened to all that Yosef shared, then said with calmness and love, "My dearest Yosef, I am proud that you were selected to represent the Sanhedrin. For a new member, that is a statement of trust. What you tell me of Gamaliel's advice seems right and proper. While I respect the report that you say that Nicodemus made, it is important that you must listen to some of the teachings of this man and make a clear unbiased judgment. The Sanhedrin are counting on you to assess any contradiction or threat to our Jewish beliefs. Then report those to the council, calmly, based solely on the facts you have found.

"Now, my dear husband if I may make one other observation. You know that I was raised from childhood in accordance with Mosaic law. I am schooled more so than many of my women friends. However, many of the laws that you and I subscribe to are situational and seem to have been required, not for worship or spiritual reasons, but for reasons of, may I say, an artificial strictness. Your example of handwashing is certainly of practical and health matters, but as a religious law, I wonder."

Yosef nodded in agreement, thinking *she does express herself clearly and well*. So, over the next several weeks, even as he struggled with his own questions, he sought out gatherings of the rabbi in Jerusalem and surrounding villages. He would stand on the fringe of crowds listening to the teachings, but what he was hearing was not contrary to most of what he believed. The most damning element seemed, to Yosef, to be this matter of loving everyone, even when it violated some of the sacred laws and long-held biases. A good example would be, how does one love a hated Samaritan? That is an idea too hard to accept, or simply to understand.

He had even seen what appeared to him to be an act of healing, and on the Sabbath, no less! It wasn't the healing. It was the day on which it occurred. And it wasn't that the Carpenter was teaching anything in direct opposition to Sanhedrin thought. What was most troubling to him was how strongly people were attracted to what he was teaching.

More and more people were becoming followers of this man. In the eyes of the Sanhedrin, that could mean trouble in the future.

It was then he recalled something that Nicodemus had said during the heated discussion. The Pharisee said that he had gone to the rabbi and, what did he say? Yes, he remembered, he had said that what the man was teaching was too unorthodox and mysterious to follow! Yosef wondered, if he now disagreed with that. He found himself furthered conflicted, because from what he had heard from the rabbi, it didn't seem unorthodox nor mysterious, in fact, at one level it made positive sense.

Finally, he decided, it was time to seek out Gamaliel and get his perspectives on all of this, and, suddenly, he found he was at war with himself. Would it appear that he was disloyal to the belief structure of the Saducees if we found favor with anything from the rabbi? Which brought another thought, maybe he did have some conflict with their strict interpretation of sacred writ. Once again, he considered talking with his old teacher about these concerns, if the opportunity presented itself.

It was a few days later that Yosef was able to meet with Gamaliel. He expressed to his elder that he was not sure what he would say to the Sanhedrin. He allowed that some of what Nicodemus had said did make sense, that what the rabbi was teaching did seem too easy, too simplistic. But he was not sure it was so much mysterious as simply a different perspective on certain elements of Mosaic law.

Gamaliel listen carefully to all the young Saducee had to say, nodding in agreement to many points. Finally, he asked Yosef, "Do you believe in your heart that this rabbi poses a threat to Judaism? If your answer is yes, then that is what you must report. If you do not believe in your heart that this rabbi poses a threat to Judaism, into the future, then, that too, is what you must report. I trust your judgment on this matter."

Eventually, the Sanhedrin was reconvened, and Yosef stood before them, and gave his report. At length, he expressed his honest opinion that, while the rabbi spoke in opposition to some elements of Mosaic law, overall, the teaching of this man posed no threat to Judaism and our understanding of holy writ. He did recognize that much of what the rabbi was teaching seemed to be popular, but, in his opinion, overall, it was much too simple, had no substance, such as The Law, and posed no threat to Judaism.

Yosef's report, while serious and represented his true understandings, nevertheless, a significant portion of the Sanhedrin was not convinced. Opposition to the "mad rabbi" continued to fester. It would be later when opposition got more and more outspoken and sparked violence within the city of Jerusalem, that grumbling among the Sanhedrin, turned to a call for action.

All of this would be brought to a head in a few months, during Passover Week, when Jesus of Nazareth, claiming that he was acting under the authority of God, single-handedly drove out the money changers and sellers of animals, from the temple, shutting down the operation and calling the Sadducees, a wicked and adulterous generation, and a "brood of vipers!"

Chapter 16

GADARA

Meanwhile, in Scythopolis, Shimon was awake early on this travel day. His time in the beautiful city had been both profitable and enjoyable, but it had also given him cause to wonder about the stories he had heard of the carpenter-rabbi. Yet, it was with anticipation of completing this market journey, that he reset the harness on the mule and put in place the much lighter cargo baskets. He then saddled his horse, took one last look around the stable, and was on his way, knowing he would be in Gadara by afternoon.

The trail along the east side of the Jordan was easy to follow, with few fellow travelers. On the other hand, across the river, many groups of pilgrims, which Shimon assumed were heading to Jerusalem for the week of Passover festivities.

By late morning, as expected, he was approaching the banks of the Jabbok Creek, where it flowed into the Jordan. Shimon smiled for he knew that just east, a mile or so, was the town of Gadara. He was hoping that tomorrow would be a good market day and soon after he would be on his way home to Tirzah. While he was happy to travel to these markets, it always made him glad to realize the profit he had made, but also the relief of being finished.

The Jabbok Valley was such a beautiful place. So, different from the browns of the barren desert of his travels from Samaria. He easily crossed the stream, not yet at spring flood stage, and into rolling hills of vineyards and olive trees, so green, it almost hurt his eyes. The town of Gadara would be just beyond this next rise.

With anticipation, he urged his horse and mule up the hill, then, just as he reached the crest, he stopped and blinked in wonder. There, before him, was a scene that challenged his mind. He could not believe his eyes. It was just amazing! He looked around and realized that he stood on the far side of a rock-strewn hillside, shaped like an amphitheater.

What was he seeing? Crowds of people. *What are they doing here?* Some were in obvious family groups, children, and adults, sitting on the ground. While still others sat on, or leaned against the many large stones that dotted the hillside. Hundreds of people. No, more. Too numerous for him to count. He stared, dazed, trying to convince himself that he was seeing this! He had never seen such a crowd. He was sure there were more people here than lived in Tirzah.

It was now early afternoon. Almost everyone was seated, most were quiet and attentive and, yet, somehow, it seemed they were all animated, smiling, some were crying, many embracing one another. He could plainly see a mix of excitement and calm on their faces.

His gaze took in the whole hillside, and, there, at the bottom of the hill, at the edge of the Jabbok Creek, a man stood speaking to them, in a voice that was warm and friendly. He could tell that most of the people were listening to him. Interesting. *Who was this man?*

He looked around, not knowing what to do. *Should I leave?* The main gate to the town was on the other side. No, he wanted to stay, and he had a feeling he was welcome. Besides, he was curious. He wanted to know where all these people had come from? What had drawn them here, in this somewhat remote place? It had to be the man who was speaking. *Who was that? What was he saying?*

On his travels, he had seen hundreds of Jewish pilgrims, families, and individuals, on their way to Jerusalem for the Passover festivities. They had been animated and excited. But he didn't think the people he was seeing here on this hillside, were pilgrims, and he didn't think many were Jews, at least from their dress.

Shimon urged his horse and mule slowly up the hill and around the top of the amphitheater, behind the crowd, until he found a place to tether his animals. He then sat down and listened to the man speaking from the edge of the river. He was surprised at how well he could understand every word that was being said, despite the distance to the creek.

He realized the man was talking in little stories, parables, that had meaning. Lessons on how to live a good life, being friendly to others, showing compassion, seeing others as, what did he call them, neighbors, yes. Hmmm, what a good thought. *I like what he's saying*, Shimon thought. After a while, he turned to the man who sat nearby and asked, "Who is that man? Everyone seems to be listening to everything he is saying. And who are these people? How long have you been here?"

The man looked at him, then, pointing to the bottom of the hill, he said in a hushed voice, "You do not know who that is? That is Jesus. He is from Galilee, and he is a great and powerful teacher. From what he has taught us, we believe he is truly a man of God."

Shimon was stunned! His mind was suddenly spinning! *That was Jesus? The one they called a rabbi or a carpenter, and now a man of God. That man from Pella, who told of his experience up north, of a crowd being feed, had said the teacher's name was Jesus.* He sat there trying to think, his mind overwhelmed. *Could this be the one in all those made-up stories and fables I have been hearing? If he is, what does that mean? He's such an ordinary looking man, no different from me, except younger.*

"And these people?" the man next to him interrupted his thinking, "These people have come from all over Gilead, parts of Ammon and as far north as Gaulanitis just to hear him teach and tell stories and lessons that have meaning for all of us. Some of us have been following along with him for days. I'm here from Beth-shan, just on the other side of the Jordan, but, my friends, sitting over there, came from northern Decapolis, beyond the city of Hippos, three day's journey. And there are a few Jewish pilgrims who have joined us, on their way to Jerusalem for the Passover celebration. But mostly, we are Gentiles and a few from Greece."

Shimon nodded a thanks to the man and then settled himself, his mind still in turmoil. *What was he to think? It was one thing to hear stories told secondhand, it's another to sit here and listen to the very man the stories gave credit to. This is ridiculous! Those stories were impossible! Miracles, that defied his own ability to think.* Yet here he sat. *I'll stay and listen for just bit, but I need to get on and check into the Inn and get my animals settled.* So, he continued to listen to this Jesus of Nazareth, the one they called the carpenter, or was he a rabbi?

Chapter 17

A MIRACLE?

By late afternoon, Shimon still sat on the hill looking down to the Jabbok Creek, listening to Jesus of Nazareth. His horse and mule contentedly grazing on the grass behind him.

His mind still trying to grasp what is before him, his thoughts a jumble. *It's like the traveler from Pella said, what this man was teaching made so much sense.* Shimon found himself agreeing. He continued to sit there mesmerized by what he was hearing and seeing. *So, this is the rabbi, who may be a carpenter, but who obviously is an excellent teacher? Maybe, if I have a chance, I could ask him about the lepers,* he thought. No, he then realized that he didn't really want to know, to confirm the healing would change too many things, he would rather not face that right now.

It was getting late, and he was aware of being hungry. He studied Jesus, who seemed to be offering a blessing of sorts. He had a small loaf of bread in one hand and a small piece of something, fish probably, in the other. Interesting. *What's he doing?*

As Shimon watched, Jesus put the fish and bread in a basket and on his lap and handed it to one of his followers. Then he handed another basket to another one of his followers. *Wait a minute! Where did that second basket come from?* Then there was a third. As he watched in amazement, basket after basket began to circulate over the hillside, and he marveled at what he was seeing. *How could this be? How did he do that?*

The man next to him, tapped him on the arm. "Are you watching? Did you see what he did, just now? I cannot believe what I'm seeing, there before us. Are you watching? Can you see what is happening? I think it is a miracle! Yes, in our very presence, he has done a miraculous thing."

"Yes, I was watching. It's like he offered a prayer or a blessing, and then those baskets, where did they all come from?" Shimon asked in unbelief. "What is he doing? Who are those men handing out more baskets? I don't understand. Not a miracle, it's a trick, an amazing trick."

"They must be his disciples. It is not a trick, my friend. Yes, he blessed the food, but I do believe we are all experiencing a miracle! Just look. Are you watching? Do you see?" the man said, pointing. "Yes, I am sure those are his disciples, but, I agree, where did those baskets come from?"

The two watched in disbelief as more baskets made their way throughout the crowd.

"I believe that Jesus has provided food; bread and fish, for all of us, for all these people," the man gestured across the crowd. "Look. Do you not see all that is happening? It's a miracle, my friend. It's a miracle!"

Shimon could only look out over the crowd in silence. He could see more baskets being passed, all over the hillside, and he recalled the words of that man from Pella, *"He fed us! Thousands and thousands of people, there on the hillside and he fed us!"*

The man continued, "Those baskets, they must all be filled with bread and fish. I don't know how this happened. I only know that after three days any food we brought, for our travels, was gone and this crowd could no longer get food in Gadara. So, all of us are hungry.

"We must remember this. We saw Jesus took a small amount of food, that someone had brought, blessed it, and there, before us, were baskets, baskets of food, now being passed. Do you see them?"

"You keep saying that. Of course, I can see, but there has got to be some trick to this," Shimon said in wonder and disbelief.

"A trick? Listen, stranger, we had nothing. We did not come prepared to stay this long. Gadara has no more food to sell. Now, as you can see, he is feeding us with bread and fish, and, of course, his words. It truly is a miracle. There is no doubt he is a man of God and we; we all have been blessed. You think it's a trick? You have seen it with your own eyes. Yet, you do not believe?"

Shimon shook his head in wonder and disbelief. He looked at the man, then out over the crowd. "Are you serious? A miracle? Come, now, there must be an explanation for this," he said without conviction. At that moment, his own words came to him, *'unless I see it with my own eyes, those things you have called a miracle, I just won't believe any of it.'* Well, he had seen it with his own eyes. Why was he having a hard time believing it?"

Just then, a basket was handed to him. He gripped it by the handle and realized it was heavy, and, yes, it was filled with bread and fish. He was hungry, so, without thinking about it, he reached in and took out a good quantity.

Having taken his food, he started to pass the basket on to another. Then, he stopped, looked into the basket, then at the food he had taken, there in his lap. The basket was still full! He sat there, transfixed in amazement, looking, first to the basket still full, and then, to all the fish he still held in his hand and the small loaf of bread he had placed on his lap. *How could this be? This happened here, I took food with my own hand. The basket is still full.*

The man had said it was a miracle, but Shimon didn't know what to make of all this. He had doubts, and yet, what is this, if not a miracle, what then? If a trick, how could this have been done? You don't make food and baskets out of thin air. There has got to be more to this. But he had no answer. Just shook his head, in wonder and amazement.

Even as the basket was taken from him, the man who had spoken to him, turned, and nodded toward Jesus, saying, "We, you and I, and all these others, are all part of a miracle. Remember this, my friend. You are a witness to a miracle by a man of God, Jesus of Nazareth."

Shimon could only nod, but thought, "*That's the carpenter. That's the rabbi. That's the one they tell tales about. That's the one I have doubts and questions about. This scene and the one he heard about two days ago, up north, was like so many of those stories he had heard, stories told as if they were true, but he had wondered if they were just fairy tales. Yet, what had he just* seen? Did he taste a miracle? How could this have happened? Yet, thousands on this hillside, all seemed to have had their fill.

What had he, himself, said just yesterday? The words were right there, fresh in his mind: *Feeding a crowd from what? Nothing, nothing at all. I couldn't believe something like that unless I saw it with my very own eyes.* With my own eyes. As if in answer to my own doubts.

His thoughts returned to the dining room in Scythopolis, and the story told by that man from Pella. What he had described was what Shimon had just experienced. It wasn't just the baskets of food, it was what the man down there by the river had talked about and how it affected the people here, on this hillside. It was all of this, taken together, that had such an effect on that man. And now? *What is happening to me?*

It was in those other stories, that Shimon had heard of the man from Nazareth, and it was here on this hillside that he heard the name of the man, Jesus. But it was not just the name, he heard him teach, and so much more. Jesus of Nazareth, carpenter, and teacher. Yet people were calling him a miracle worker, a man of God. How unbelievable is that?

He sat there, eating, and watching baskets of food circulating among the crowd, until everyone had been fed. He was stunned, wondering if Jesus, was truly responsible. This was not a story, but there must be a trick, somehow. This was not magic. It was something made up to fool the crowd. This was something he saw and touched and tasted and witnessed. Yes, he had witnessed all this, why was he still not convinced it was a miracle? Still, how did it really happen?

Despite the doubt that crowded his mind, he could not deny what he had seen, what he had touched. That man, standing there in front of this crowd, *who is he, really?* Had he succeeded in tricking this large group, one way or another? This was like those stories he heard and doubted on his journey. Were any of them true, or just tricks? Despite having witnessed the reality of what happened on this hillside, he continued to be plagued with doubt that this, or any of the stories, were true. And, there again, in his mind, that pesky little phrase, what if…? What if he had just witnessed a miracle? Why was he denying what he had seen? What he had tasted.

He stayed on the edge of the crowd where he could see and still hear the man. Yes, the man looked a bit like a carpenter. He had a kind face. When he spoke, it was with such confidence and compassion, and authority. Shimon thought with a smile that with that talent, he should be a salesman.

Again, he thought, yes, he spoke with authority, as if he knew, really knew that what he was saying was true. He talked about love and mercy and having compassion for your neighbor. And it was clear from what he was saying that a neighbor was anyone. It didn't matter who that person was, or what that person believed, God loved him, and God wanted us to love him, as well. I like that, Shimon thought, then immediately rejected it. No, no! Don't be a fool. Come on, there are some that you could not possibly love. People who wanted to hurt you, to kill you.

Could I love a Jew? Love them? They have wealth and they buy lots of my goods, but they can be dangerous! Could I ever love them? I don't think so.

What was hard to accept, he said to himself, *was that when the "carpenter" spoke about God, it was as if God really was his father, his loving father! Huh. Imagine that! There was this Jesus telling them, that God was their father as well, and that they were loved. What a good thought, but… Really? God loves me?*

These were things that Shimon had never thought about, and right now he was having a hard time getting those thoughts out of his mind. It wasn't as if he wanted those thoughts out of his mind, no, he wanted to know more about what it meant. But he never… Never, what? *Finally,* he told himself, *I don't know. I've got to think about this. It is too much!*

Most of the crowd was leaving, some headed toward the Creek and on to the Jordan River, on their way to Jericho and Jerusalem, while others were making their way toward the inn. That reminded him that he needed to get moving himself and get his animals settled.

Then he noticed the disciples, moving around the hillside picking up baskets with bits of food remaining. Fascinated, he watched for a while, and wondered what they would do with those blessed leftovers. There seemed to be a lot.

Chapter 18

A TRICK!

He continued to sit on the hillside breathing deeply of the fresh air and allowed his mind to repeatedly replay what he had seen and heard. Loving others was a new, foreign idea for him. There had been so many others that he had not loved. Times when he took advantage of people when he turned his back to other's needs.

He thought about his dear friend, Nahman, the one he had almost lost because of an argument. No, not an argument, a time when he insisted on being dishonest, and rather than admit he was wrong, he had lost control! His friend had walked away, but now they had reconciled and had become partners in the shop. He felt at peace about that.

He thought about what the rabbi had said about loving others, and forgiveness. *Yes, forgiveness had mended the breach in their friendship. When I am home, I must tell him all about what I have heard and seen…and tasted!*

This is ridiculous! Why am I thinking this way? Some people just naturally deserve to be cheated, or they have wealth, and they were not very smart. Enough of this stuff! I can't let being good to people hurt my business, can I? I'm not giving my goods away, just to be kind. Yet, he knew he had been changing, ever so slowly, over the past several months. Something was happening and he didn't know what. What about this? What this man had said and the miracle he had witnessed? He wondered. *Now I'm calling it a miracle!*

After a time, most everyone had left the hillside. He gathered himself and led his animals toward the stable and the inn, surprised to find he was in conflict between all that he had heard recently and what he had believed all his life.

He had a thought: *Did he really regret, how he had treated others? Maybe, just a little. Certainly, his friend. Did he regret cheating others? Why would he regret business transactions? After all, buyer beware.* He had to smile, even he wasn't convinced in the truth of that little misleading cliché. Still, he admitted to himself, he was not always honest, and he had misrepresented some of his goods, some of his dealings.

Strange, where did those thoughts come from, he asked himself? Why would I regret any of my business? All this talk about loving others was driving him to distraction, which caused him to smile! *Maybe distraction is good?* Still, he smiled, while those thoughts persisted. Good thoughts.

He took his animals to the stable and arranged for feed and security. Then he walked to the inn, deep in thought, wondering about all that he had heard and seen.

He could not help recalling what had been told to him in Scythopolis, days before, a similar "miracle" there in Bethsaida. And now this experience. In his mind, he thought he knew the truth. Some stories were just stories. *This man could not have turned water into wine. Or had He?* Some stories were built around what had occurred, just naturally. So, he probably had not actually healed lepers. *This man had not actually fed this crowd, including himself, on this hill, or any other. Just tricks! Although I ate the food and it was good, and I can't figure out the trick! Stop thinking that way.*

That is where his reasoning stopped. But *how could what he heard, saw and tasted, not be true? I was there! Why am I denying my own eyes? Who was this man? Was he a master of tricks, or a holy man?* The words of Jesus still echoed in his mind. Good words, holy words, loving words. *I've got to stop thinking like this.*

When Shimon arrived at the inn, people were talking excitedly about their experience on the hill. He sat at a table in the dining room, and listened for a time to what was being said around him. Then he turned to a man nearby and asked what he thought.

The man replied, "This Jesus, is a man of God. He is truly a prophet. What he teaches was sent by God. His message really touched me. And then, the bread and the fish…a blessing, a miracle!"

"You really believe that? Yes, I liked what he was teaching, but the feeding. Don't you see that it must be an elaborate trick of some kind?"

"You can't be serious. If you had been there on the hillside, you wouldn't say that!"

"I was there, and I saw what happened. I ate some of the food. I don't know how he did it, but I must believe that it was a trick!"

"You were there and saw what happened and, yet you still doubt? What is wrong with you? Well, believe what you want. I heard his message, and I witnessed the miracle that he caused, and I believe this Jesus is a holy man. I wish I could stay another day and hear more of his teaching, but tomorrow I must begin the long journey north to my home."

Shimon had nothing more to say yet doubts still bothered him. Yes, his message had been powerful, but the conflict was still there. Was it a miracle or a trick? Maybe I'll listen to more of what he has to say, tomorrow. Without another word, he simply turned away, and looked at the board that displayed the menu, but realized that he was not hungry. It seemed that the taste of that bread and fish from Jesus was still on his tongue and on his mind. Still conflicted, he left the dining room, and stepped outside. The evening air was cool and welcoming, and he felt himself calming down. He needed to concentrate on preparations for tomorrow's market. Tomorrow's market. Would he have customers, or would they all be gathered on the hillside to hear this…what? Carpenter? Rabbi? Holy Man? Who, indeed?

Chapter 19

CHANGE OF PLANS

When Shimon arrived at the marketplace the next morning his early fears were realized when he saw how few customers were lined up at his stall. He asked the man in charge of the marketplace about that, "I know, I'm disappointed, as well. Let me tell you, tomorrow should be much better. Word was out about that Rabbi, with the crowd that was following him, and so merchants, like you, have agreed to come a day later, and I think that applies to customers as well. It's amazing how that information gets out. Listen to me, tomorrow will be better, just wait and see."

"But", Shimon said, a little exasperated, "the rabbi will still be here, along with that crowd of followers, so, it won't be any different."

"Ah, not so. That man from Galilee, that you call a rabbi, left early this morning. One of his followers told me they are going to Jericho tonight, and then, in a day or two, they will continue to Bethany. Apparently, he plans to be in Jerusalem for the week of Passover. Maybe he will be teaching in the Temple. I must tell you; I am happy to be rid of that group."

Shimon was surprised at the mixed emotions he felt in learning that Jesus had left. He pondered that for a while, then turned his attention to setting up his stall, with the hope of enough customers to make it worthwhile. Throughout the day, sales were slow and customers few, and, while he sold some of his store of goods, by day's end, he decided to wait another day, on the hope of selling all his remaining goods, and his mule.

However, by mid-afternoon of the following day, he still had a supply of spices and bolts of silk cloth. He struggled with the thought that he would need to travel to Jericho, to sell the few things he had left. That would also mean returning home by way of Jerusalem, a risky journey during this time of Jewish celebrations.

Shimon stepped outside the marketplace, trying to decide what to do. He thought about setting up his stall for another day, in hopes of selling out his goods here, but thought that two days at the Gadara market was enough.

From where he was standing, he looked out over the green of the valley, and the rolling hills of vineyards. He had been admiring this scene since he came here and realized he had another idea, one that appealed to him. Why not visit some of those vineyards and give himself a break from the marketplace? Besides, he now had room in his cargo baskets for jugs or skins of wine.

He returned to the Inn, extended his stay, and inquired about wineries of the area. Over the next two days, he toured several, enjoying samples and making purchases. It was an enjoyable and restful break from his travels. By the end of his second day, he had added eight skins of freshly made wine. With a smile, he was confident that he could sell several of the skins, make a little profit, and retain one or two for his own enjoyment. He felt…what? Happy? Yes, and at peace.

So, since he now had the wine and some of his goods, he would make the journey to Jericho. He reasoned that in a few days, Passover week would be nearly over, and this might be a good plan. So, it was with renewed hope, that, in the morning, he packed up and made his way on to Jericho.

Chapter 20

TROUBLE

Now it was less than a week before the start of the Jewish Festival of Unleavened Bread, or Passover. A rabbi from the synagogue in Beersheba, Meir Kahane, began the trek to Bethany, on the hillside of Mount of Olives, near Jerusalem. He was excited to make this journey because he was the newly appointed rabbi, to the synagogue in Jericho, and he would be there just in time to celebrate Passover. His plan was to meet a member of the Jerusalem Sanhedrin, in Bethany, an honor that made him smile. They would travel together, down the rugged and dangerous road to Jericho. He had never been to the city, and certainly had never travelled that road. It would be an adventure!

The travel, so far, had been easy, and he and his companion made good time, the horses they rode had been sure-footed without mishap. They arrived in Hebron, right on schedule, where they would spend the night and enjoy food and comfortable lodging. Their plan was to leave the next morning, make their way through Bethlehem, south of Jerusalem, and arrive in Bethany, to meet with the member of the Sanhedrin. Then, together, they would journey to Jericho. Yes, it would be an interesting journey.

Trouble began the next morning, when their horses were nowhere to be found, and to make matters worse, their cargo bags, packed with clothing and supplies, were also missing. Other travelers smiled that these strangers from Beersheba had not taken better care to secure their animals and their supplies. They should have known about the thieves that recently plagued visitors to Hebron.

The rabbi consulted with officials of the Hebron synagogue and determined that they could provide priestly garb, but they had no horses or mules available. He was informed that the synagogue in the town of Herodium, a half-day's journey on foot, did have mules they could provide. After sending a messenger on to Bethany to alert them to the delay, they began their walk to obtain animals for the remainder of their journey.

Even as the rabbi was on his way to Herodium, the merchant from Samaria stood on the bank of the Jordan River, deciding where to cross. He had been here before, but the river was nearing flood stage, and while the boundaries of the Jabbok fjord were clearly visible, he needed to take care. Finally, he urged his horse into the flow and crossed, leading the mule. Once on the other side, he turned toward Jericho and continued his journey. He would be in Jericho by mid-afternoon.

In Herodium, early the next day, Rabbi Kahane, and his companion, now with new provisions, rode borrowed mules out of the village in the direction of Bethany. They would arrive there, late morning, and hopefully begin their travels on to Jericho, yet that day.

Meanwhile, in Jerusalem, preparations were well underway for the Week of Passover. The sun had just crested the eastern horizon, dawn of a fresh new day. Yosef, his beard well-trimmed, dressed in expensive, clerical robes, and wearing hand-tooled sandals, was emerging from the temple in Jerusalem. From his belt hung a fringed leather satchel. In his hand, he carried a heavy, elaborately decorated, staff. He looked the part of Jewish aristocracy and authority.

Yosef, representing the Sanhedrin, was on a mission, first to Bethany and then on to Jericho. The satchel he carried contained an allotment of silver for the Temple in Jericho, in support of their Passover celebration. He was not in a good frame of mind. While this mission had been assigned in the spirit of trust, in his mind, he could not shake the feeling that this 'honor' was an expression of their displeasure and disagreement with his report, months before.

With the temple behind him, he walked through Damascus Gate, turned east, toward Bethany, into the dawn of a new day. In Bethany, he would meet a rabbi that would accompany him on the journey to Jericho. However, when he arrived, he learned that the rabbi, traveling from Beersheba, had been delayed, and would arrive later in the day or, possibly, the next.

Despite not knowing what may have delayed the rabbi, he became angry and thought it was irresponsible of the man. He had not wanted to make this journey, in the first place. This was an errand for a Sadducee of lessor stature, yet, he had consented. So, he fumed.

He debated whether he should return to Jerusalem or proceed, as planned. The road to Jericho was steep and rugged, but he knew it well, and had traveled this way many times before. He considered the dangers of this road but thought he could handle anything that happened. Again, he debated, what to do? Travelling alone was risky, but he had great confidence in himself. It was early, he reasoned. If he hurried, he could be in Jericho by nightfall, if not, he could spend a night in Wadi Qelt. Was it foolhardy to set off alone, or should he wait?

Common sense prevailed, and he decided to wait until morning, surely the rabbi would have arrived by then. So, Yosef retraced his steps home, thinking that if, in the morning he is not here, well, again, he had great confidence in himself, and his staff, he would travel this way alone.

Early the next day, Yosef, returned to Bethany and found himself angry once again because the missing rabbi still had not arrived. Leaving word that he would proceed on to Jericho, he turned and left Bethany, with quick, confident steps, made his way north. Now, with the Mount of Olives at his back, he started down the steep road to Jericho. He reasoned, if he stayed on pace, he could easily be in Jericho by nightfall.

Sometime later, he passed an inn, nodded to the innkeeper, sitting on a bench just outside the door. It was too early for his midday meal; besides he carried food with him. He paused for a brief rest, asked the man if there had been other travelers.

"So far, you are the first," the innkeeper replied, walking over to him. "Are you traveling alone? Brave man," he said, but thought, *foolish man*. "We have some good food, and I am sure that my niece would be happy to prepare a lunch for you to take on the road, should you be interested."

Yosef looked toward the innkeeper and noticed a young woman, standing in the doorway of the Inn. "No," he said, "I must be on my way." Then he stood and, with a nod and a wave of his hand, he picked up his brisk pace and continued down the road.

"He is traveling alone?" the woman asked, stepping over to where her uncle stood. "It's not safe to be alone on this road. Was he a priest? Pretty fancy for a traveler"

"That is true, Mara, it is not safe. He is one foolish man. He wears his wealth, for all to see. There is trouble in store for that man," the innkeeper predicted.

The niece nodded in agreement, and said, "Well, I hope he makes the journey without incident. We will soon have more Pilgrims coming up the road to Jerusalem for Passover, which means I should get busy in the kitchen." Then, together, they returned to the Inn.

Chapter 21
A PERFECT DAY

Yosef maintained his brisk pace for several hours, making good time. Then, after he carefully negotiated an especially steep stretch, the road leveled off, and he paused to rest. His feet hurt from the stones and gravel of the road, and he sat for a time on a large stone. *I don't recall this road being so rugged,* he thought.

After a few minutes, he stood and walked to the edge of the road, admiring the broad expanse of the Jordan valley below. He could see all the way down to the river, glistening like a silver ribbon in the sunlight. On the far side of the valley, he could just make out a patch of green, and the movement of a small herd of animals. No longer angry, he smiled. The sky was blue with few clouds, and the day was cool, so unlike yesterday. He thought, *what a perfect day to make this journey*!

He turned his thoughts to the role he would play in the synagogue in Jericho during the week of Passover. Apart from the ceremony of presenting the Passover support to the senior rabbi, he had no doubt that he would be asked to play a significant part in various events. He looked forward to blessing those people with his teaching. People would notice him, he thought with a smile. Maybe making this journey could turn into a good thing for him.

Suddenly, he was struck on his head from behind! In surprise, he staggered to regain his balance, to keep from falling into the valley. He turned and lifted his staff to protect himself from the unseen aggressor. As he did, he was struck on his shoulder, this time from the other side and realized there were two attackers. He started to strike out with his staff, when he was hit again on the head, dazed, and knocked to the ground. Before he could do anything, he was hit again, and again and then, everything went black.

Three men quickly stripped Yosef of his outer tunic and his robe. They took his sandals and the ornate staff. They talked excitedly when they discovered the satchel that held the temple allotment. They couldn't believe their good fortune and paused to divide the silver pieces among themselves. When they started to roll the body off the edge of the road, one of the men realized that people were coming down the road, and yelled, "Leave the body! Let's get out of here, people are coming!" All three turned and hurried down the road, toward Jericho, leaving Yosef, where he lay. It was no longer a perfect day.

While the attack on Yosef was happening, Rabbi Kahane and his aid finally arrived in Bethany, late morning only to be informed that the person they were to meet, had gone on ahead earlier that day. The rabbi was deeply concerned, because neither he nor his companion had traveled the road down to Jericho. The dilemma of what to do, was solved when a Levite arrived and announced that he had traveled this road many times and was going to Jericho to participate in the sacred services of Passover.

So, with instruction and prayers from the Levite, the party of three, began their descent north, their over-night destination would be Wadi Qelt, just five miles from the city of Jericho. They made a brief stop at the Inn, to obtain food for their evening meal. They inquired of the young woman at the inn about travelers on the road, and she told them there had been a steady flow of pilgrims coming up the road, heading for Jerusalem, but, to her knowledge, only one man was traveling down the road to Jericho, that was very early, and he was alone.

Later in the afternoon, the small group, led by the Levite, approached the nearly naked, beaten body of Yosef, lying on the side of the road. They paused, looked at the body, then to one another, debating what to do. They had no way of knowing who the man might be. Suddenly, they looked around, fearful that the robbers might still be nearby. Rabbi Kahane, shook his head, not wanting to touch the "dead body" and making it obvious that he wanted to be on his way. The Levite then settled the matter, stating that they should not be on this road after dark, and pointing to the other side of the road, led them around "the body" and on their way.

Chapter 22

ON TO JERICHO

Three days before, Shimon, having left Gadara early that morning, paused at the edge of the Jordan River, and studied the current, rushing over the fjord, just north of where the Jabbok Creek flowed into the Jordan. He had made this crossing years before, but that was when there was no threat of flood.

This was early spring. It had been a hard winter in the upper Jordan Valley, with heavy rains and melting snows, now flowing south, into the Sea of Galilee, then on to the lower valley causing the river to be near flood stage. At flood levels, the rushing river could threaten towns along its banks down to Gilgal, just north of Jericho, and in the process, damaging several of the fjords along the way.

His horse and mule seemed disinterested, or bored, and now they grazed on the lush grass at river's edge. Through the rushing water, Shimon could barely make out the blurred outer boundaries of the fjord, increasing the risk of crossing. He would need to use great care, because of the depth of the water and the force of the current. Still, he was confident that, with care, it would not be a problem.

Letting his animals rest and graze, Shimon looked up at the high ridges that framed the Jordan Valley, jagged teeth against the blue of the sky. The surrounding hills were uninviting, various shades of tans and browns, rough, rock-strewn, and treacherous. The valley was nearly devoid of trees or bushes, and the only grass was that growing at river's edge. From his previous journey, he knew the road on the other side of the river was well-traveled, and level. He recalled that the land that lay above the valley, around Jerusalem and beyond, was lush and green.

His immediate concern was there, along the valley. His travels had been uneventful, so far. He had yet to see any wildlife, nor many of the venomous snakes common to this region, but he remained alert. What worried him most would be the ill-tempered Oryx, with its long, curved, sharp horns. He knew it was a dangerous animal, one that would charge a traveler without provocation.

His mind played again his experience there on the hillside of Gadara. *Yes, the feeding of all those people had been an amazing experience, but more important,* as Shimon thought about it, *was what that rabbi had taught -- lessons that were so powerful, about life and relationships.* These were ideas that he had never considered, yet he saw how they could change a person's life.

He smiled when he thought about those stories he had first heard about a carpenter. *A carpenter of all things! The title, rabbi, fit the man better. But what had the man called him last evening at dinner? A man of God, that was it. Maybe he is a holy man, maybe he isn't.* Shimon didn't know, but he would think about that later.

He looked again at the current, rushing by in front of him. On the other side, he could see a few houses and shops in the village of Gilgal, and he knew, once he crossed, he would be in Jericho before nightfall. Overall, it had been an exhausting journey and he wanted nothing more than a good meal at the Inn and a night's rest. While he was not a Jew, he was aware that the grand celebration of Passover would begin in a few days, so he knew that there would be much activity in town. He hoped he would not have trouble getting a room, or a place to feed and stable his horse and mule.

His thoughts were interrupted by his horse pawing the ground, as if to remind him that it was time to cross the Jordan. The rider agreed, took another look at the fast-moving current over the fjord, determined the boundaries for safe passage, then slowly urged his horse forward, leading the mule, moving carefully through the flood. Safe on the other side, and with a sigh of relief, he turned south, skirting Gilgal, and then, following the river, onward toward Jericho.

From his experience, he knew that the market in Jericho was small, but of good reputation and selective, so he was confident that he could sell the few remaining goods he carried. He knew that the skins of wine would command a good price. He also hoped that he could sell his mule and the accompanying cargo harness.

Once all that was completed, then, he would begin the real challenge, the assent up the very difficult and dangerous road to Bethany. It would be a hard climb for man and horse, especially the first few miles. He had made this seventeen-mile journey once before, a few years ago, so he had some idea what was ahead for him.

But, for now, Jericho. Shimon liked the old city. He recalled his last visit, when he was reminded several times that Jericho was the oldest city in the world, the city of Joshua. He smiled at the memory and the fact that he would hear that again, and how this town was the gateway to the promised land, the land promised to Israel by God, an oft repeated phrase.

He remembered that on the walls of the Inn were tapestries that informed all that this was the place where 'Joshua was told by God: *"No one will be able to stand up against you all the days of your life. As I was with Moses, so I will be with you; I will never leave you nor forsake you,"* Book of Joshua, second section of the Torah.' There was one beautiful tapestry that depicted the nation of Hebrews in the act of crossing the river, staking claim to the promised land.

Yes, he would see and hear all that again. It was a source of pride and spiritual strength for the citizens of Jericho. Shimon had only skimmed the Torah, and he knew little of the Hebrew Bible, but he was sure that passage was written in there, somewhere. Yes, I'll hear all that, again, probably over dinner, he thought with a smile. Small price to pay for good food and friendly company.

One of the features that attracted him to Jericho was the Inn, and especially the wonderful food in the dining room.. The marketplace was small but well-situated, near the Inn and the town square. Then there was Eisha's Spring, just on the out-skirts of town, that gushed the sweetest water he had ever tasted.

The stable was just outside the West Gate on the edge of Jericho, and that is where he first went to secure his horse, mule, and the remaining goods he carried. From there it would be a short distance to the Inn.

The stable owner greeted him with a jovial smile as he rode up and assured him that all would be secured. He then said, "You know, I have a very good memory for faces, and I believe that you were here not that long ago. Not last year, but maybe two years ago?"

"You are almost correct. It was three years ago, I stabled my horse here, stayed at the Inn and I had a stall there in the market," Shimon answered.

"I knew it! I never forget a face," the man said as he helped Shimon get his animals settled. Then he continued, "I must tell you about something that happened to my family just three days ago. There was a man, a teacher of sorts and his companions, that traveled from the Decapolis, up north, through towns on their way to Jerusalem. They spent the night here, in my town, stayed at the home of that tax collector, a most unpopular family. But that is another story.

"Anyway, my son, Bartimaeus, has been blind since he was born, and, on this day, as usual, was sitting just up there (pointing), by the edge of the road, near Eisha's Spring. He begs for alms so that he can eat. When people would pass, he would call out to them, in a strong voice. When this man and his followers passed by, he called out especially loud, and the crowd got upset. But that man and his group stopped.

"This stranger asked my son a rather obvious question, what did my son want? Well, instead of asking for alms, he said that he wanted to see. The stranger then asked another question, 'Do you believe I can give you sight?' My son answered, 'Yes, I believe you can.' Then the stranger said, *'Receive your sight; your faith has healed you.'* And my son, blind from birth, unable to see anything his whole life, was suddenly able to see! I swear that is what happened. His mother and I could hardly believe it. It was an amazing and joyful event. Later, I was told that man was Jesus, from that small town of Nazareth in Galilee. He must be a man of God."

There was that name again, Shimon thought, *Jesus*. Remembering the regret he had from Afula, by not talking to the dancing man that had been a leper, he said, "Where is your son? I would like to rejoice with him on his new-found sight."

"Ah, my son. You should have seen him yesterday, celebrating, running around the town, looking at flowers and everything. Last night he couldn't stop staring at his mother and me. It was a real family celebration. Then early this morning, when he learned that the man of God had left for Jerusalem, he told us he wanted to become a disciple of that rabbi, said goodbye, and started up the road to Bethany, following the man he now called his Master. I don't know when I'll see him again."

Disappointed at this news, Shimon said briskly, "Very interesting. I am most happy for you and your son." But he could not get the phrase, 'a man of God', out of his mind. Here was still another story, unverified, along with thoughts and images, stories that he had heard and then his experience on the hillside, all attributed to this "man of God," and it gave him pause.

Not wanting to continue the conversation, Shimon excused himself, explaining "Now I must be on my way to the Inn. I'll be here very early in the morning to get my goods and set up my stall in the marketplace. I hope to sell all that I have, and I would like to sell my fine mule and all the harnesses. If you know anyone who would want to buy, let me know." With that, he walked toward the Inn, thinking about the healing of that man's son, and wondering if that was just a tale or if that was another miracle by this man, Jesus. It seemed he could not get those stories out of his mind.

Chapter 23

MATTHIAS

Jericho. The town, which was usually quiet and peaceful, was filled with excitement and preparations for the week of Passover. On his way to the Inn, he strolled around the city, watching with interest all the preparations being made for the festive week. Shops lined the main street, selling everything from food to clothing, incense to silk and spices. There were sacrificial lambs and birds for sale. It was a carnival atmosphere, with bright banners, music being played on nearly every street corner, and crowds of people milling about. It was truly an exciting environment. As he neared the Inn, he hoped that there would be accommodations available, for he was looking forward to a fine meal, and a comfortable bed.

The Inn was a busy place, people coming and going, and after he examined the sleeping room that he would share with three other men, he walked into the crowded dining room, and was rewarded by the delicious aroma of food cooking. His hunger returned with a vengeance.

He was shown to a table by the window, occupied by another man. He sat down, ordered his dinner, along with a cup of wine, and relaxed with a heavy sigh. The man across from him smiled, and said, "You look like a traveler who has come a long way."

"Well, I have. I left home about eight days ago, and now, here I am at my final stop, before I head back home. I'm a merchant and this journey, how shall I describe it, has been rewarding and very interesting, I must say. Have you been traveling?"

"Well, yes, you can say that. My friends and I have been traveling, doing teaching and ministry with my master ever since we left Capernaum, more than two years ago. We have visited so many towns and villages on our travels. By the way, my name is Matthias."

"Mine is Shimon. Is your master here?"

"No, they've gone on ahead. My brothers and I stayed here in Jericho one night, then they left this morning for Bethany where a friend of ours is very ill. There is a family here that I have been talking with and they asked me to stay for a few days. I'll catch up with my master in Jerusalem."

"Matthias, you say you were teaching."

"Well, yes and no. My master does the teaching. He is a holy man, and through His ministry I have learned so much about God, and life, and I, in turn, talk with people when they have questions. The master is truly amazing. He's the teacher."

"Could I ask who your master is?"

"Surely. He is Jesus. Originally, he was from Nazareth. By trade, he's a carpenter. Built his own house, he did, in Capernaum, and that is where he now lives. But he is a man of God, and I have been a witness to his healing touch, his teaching and marveled at the miraculous things he has done. He's changing lives. I told you I was talking with a family here in Jericho. My master spent the night at the home of that family, and now, they all seem to be going through some changes."

"What kind of changes?" Shimon asked. "What questions?"

"Well, Zacchaeus is the man of the house, and he is the tax collector for this region, and you can imagine, not very well liked. His reputation affected the whole family, isolating them from the people of the town. Jesus spent the night with the family, sharing his message. By the time my master left the next morning, the man seemed to have changed, and made promises to Jesus. I was asked if I would stay and share a bit of my experience in this ministry, and so I stayed."

"You mentioned the man changed. How?"

"Oh, Shimon, the day that my master left for Bethany, I watched this man go to many in the town, explaining that he had over-charged them for taxes, then he paid them back, many times over that amount. People were stunned. It was a glorious thing to see."

"Matthias, tell me something. For over this past year, when I traveled to marketplaces, I heard stories of a holy man, stories that are hard to believe because it involved amazing things. The first story I heard was in the port of Caesarea, and it was about a man who changed water into wine at a wedding feast. Do you see what I mean? That's impossible. But there were other stories, stories of healing lepers. We all know that you cannot heal a leper. Even one about this rabbi raising a young girl back to life who had died.

"I haven't just heard stories. I was in Gadara just three days ago where I heard a holy man, apparently, your master, teaching. That evening he fed the crowd from hardly anything at all. Some thought that was a miracle. At the time, I wondered if there was a trick I was missing."

"Yes, Shimon, that was my master, Jesus. We just came from Gadara. I was there on that hillside. We had seen him do this before, up near Bethsaida. Listen, it amazed us, too, his disciples and I, just as much as it amazed you. Shimon, it was no trick. Believe me, we had no idea where those baskets came from. Not only that, for some of Jesus's followers, it frightened them. It was too--what's the word--magical for them and they walked away. Oh, they still believed that he is a man of God, but after being part of his ministry and witnessing other miracles, it was just too frightening for them. They had to return home.

"After Gadara, we talked with Jesus about what we had seen. He just smiled and asked if we believed in miracles. I didn't know how to answer that, after all we had seen. I said, I believed. But I still struggle.

"You know, Shimon, sometime ago, when we were up in Caesarea Philippi, Jesus asked us who did we say he is. None of us knew what to say until my friend Peter, just blurted out what we were all thinking, 'You are the Messiah, the Son of the living God.' That is what Peter said and that is what we believe. Let me tell you, we are still in awe! That story of turning water into wine? I wasn't with Him then, and I think only John, Andrew and maybe Peter were there at the wedding, along with Jesus' mother, Mary. As I said, I didn't see it, but I saw a remarkable change in those who were, it was like they discovered something new. Because of their reaction, I believe it happened just that way." s

"Matthias, tell me, again, the name of your master."

"Shimon, as I told you, my master is Jesus, and he is from Nazareth. Those stories you have heard, and what happened at Gadara? All true. I believe all are blessings. That is the ministry of my master, and He is a Man of God. After Bethany, we will be going into Jerusalem, and I am sure he will be teaching in the Temple.

"One more thing. All of us, all His disciples, are deeply concerned about Jesus' safety. When we were in Jerusalem last, there were people trying to stone Him to death. We left and went north into part of Samaria, then crossed the Jordan into Syria. We spent time in several villages and then we ended up in Gadara. I guess that is where you met him. We were alarmed when he said he wanted to return to Jerusalem. Peter tried to talk him out of it."

The two continued to talk through their dinners, and on into the evening, until the host came by to inform them that the dining room was closing. Matthias said he would be leaving for Bethany in the morning and would probably be there for a few days. They said goodbye, then parted.

Chapter 24

DID IT REALLY HAPPEN?

It was late evening. Shimon walked the streets of Jericho, now starting to quiet down for the night. His mind replayed his conversation with Matthias. He hardly remembered what the meal was because of the revelations told him by this man, this follower of Jesus of Nazareth.

Shimon's mind was filled with the epiphany: *He confirmed that most of the stories were true! He also said that there had been no trick in the feeding of crowds, what he had witnessed was a miracle.* Shimon hardly knew what to say. Matthias assured him that all those amazing things were not stories, they had happened through the ministry of his master, the man of God.

Shimon's mind was still in turmoil as he returned to the stable to check on his animals, making sure they had water and feed and that his goods were secure. Eventually he wandered back to the Inn and made his way to the sleeping room where he laid down. Sleep would not come until nearly dawn, as he struggled with what he believed and who Jesus was, what had happened there on the Gadara hillside, and the lessons that he taught.

He was struck by another thought: *Matthias! How did he come to meet Matthias? How was it that he would be seated at the table with this disciple of Jesus of Nazareth? And that man would share the stories of Jesus' ministry. That he would confirm the stories and the feeding and all those other happenings that sounded like fables, yet Matthias said they were true.* Again, he wondered, *how did he come to meet Matthias?* Indeed, how did that happen? There had been other seats at other tables opened for dinner. And, yet he was glad it happened.

He was awakened by the sounds of his roommates packing up and realized he had finally slept, but now it was time for him to gather his goods and open his stall. By the time he had everything organized, there were customers waiting in line and he felt he would easily sell all his remaining goods by the afternoon, including the skins of wine.

He was in the process of displaying his final array of goods when Matthias stopped by to thank him for the previous night's conversation and to let him know that he was on his way, first to Bethany and then to Jerusalem. "You know, Shimon, if you ever want to continue our discussion, I can be found either at Mary and Martha's home in Bethany, or they will know where I am. If you want to talk with others, in Jerusalem, followers of Jesus call themselves The Way. Just remember that Jesus is a man of God, listen to him when you have a chance. You would find that He is much more than a rabbi."

Shimon stood and watched the disciple walk away. He thought, *yes, I would very much like to continue our conversation.* Then he thought, *The Way seemed like a strange title to give followers of this Jesus. Perhaps, when he was done here and was near Bethany…* His thoughts were interrupted by a customer asking about a bolt of silk cloth.

He was thrilled when his final item was sold by mid-afternoon, and he returned to the stable to settle accounts. True to his word, the stableman had gotten him a fair price for his mule and the cargo harness.

Chapter 25

JERICHO ROAD

Over dinner, Shimon thought about the journey ahead for him and what it would bring. Being in Jericho and seeing all the activities in preparation for Passover made him realized even more that he was a Samaritan in the middle of a Jewish celebration. That made him anxious, and yet, he thought again of Mathias and the possibility of meeting him in Bethany. This could work out, he thought.

But now he had to focus on the journey he was about to take. He had traveled this road once before, three years ago. He knew the dangers, not just the road itself, but the fact that there were others who took advantage of solo travelers. Yet, he knew his size and strength would serve as a deterrent, and he would take care.

He reminded himself that the two days on the road would be strenuous, and difficult, and that would get him to the Mount of Olives, and Bethany. Then, there were different dangers of going into Jerusalem, avoiding crowds of pilgrims, finding where followers of Jesus would be gathering. All that gave him pause. Where could he be that would be safe, and he could hear Jesus' teaching? Certainly not in the temple!

Yes, all that is true, but his first worry would be the road; rough, steep, dangerous. On the first day of the climb, his destination would be the Wadi Qelt. The wadi was a large fissure, in the face of the valley wall. For travelers, this was a frequent stop-over because there was a freshwater spring, places for sleeping, and an area where he could tether his horse. There, he would rest, and prepare himself for the completed climb, the next day, up to Bethany and beyond.

As his thoughts returned to Bethany, he wondered if Matthias would be there, maybe at the home of Martha and Mary. Was that the family where the man that was ill lived?

What would he want to know? He was still getting used to the possibility that those stories were true. Was there more to the ministry of this Jesus of Nazareth? What could those sisters tell me?

Early the next morning, just as the sun was raising above the distant hills, and before it touched the valley floor, Shimon gathered his things, saddled his horse, and started up the road. Through the receding darkness, he studied the terrain ahead of him, a gradually steepening, narrow road, stones, and boulders everywhere. He knew it would continue to be a difficult and dangerous journey.

Yes, he knew about the difficulties of Jericho Road. He knew that it would be slow going, uphill, and rough. He also knew that there had been robberies and other dangers along the way, but he felt prepared. Once he reached Bethany, he was confident that it would be worth it. He had hoped to arrive at Wadi Qelt by late afternoon.

However, the road was more difficult than he remembered, much slower going, and treacherous, especially for his horse. There were times when he stumbled. There were times when his horse had difficulty negotiating the grade but, eventually, they kept going. He was very conscious that he was traveling alone, yet not really 'alone' for he was often surrounded by Jewish pilgrims, some with families, and that was comforting. Many times, he lent a hand, helping others, and one time he carried a child up an especially steep stretch. Indeed, the going was slow.

In time, he arrived at Wadi Qelt, just as darkness settled around him. The lights of torches were scattered around, travelers, pilgrims staying the night, as they made their way to Jerusalem for the Passover Festival.

He lit a torch and, at the spring, gave his horse water, refreshed himself, and refilled his water jar. Then he found a comfortable place where he could tether and feed his horse and safely stay the night. He took out the food he brought and settled in for his evening meal and a good rest. That night he slept well.

Chapter 26

WHO IS MY NEIGHBOR?

The morning dawned cool and clear, and Shimon, staying focused, was on his way, just as the sun was reflecting on the upper reaches of the Jordan valley. He was first on the road this day, but others would follow. Leading his horse up steep grades, the road continued to be difficult, but he still hoped to reach Bethany, on Mount of Olives, by the end of the day.

The events of the last several days were never far from his mind. *Do I really have an answer to all those stories, all of those 'what ifs?'* Most of the doubts that he had carried around were being overshadowed by a growing conviction that this Jesus of Nazareth was much more than a rabbi. If he accepts that Jesus is a man of God, and is the Messiah, then there was no conflict, just another question, what's next? In his heart, he knew that the answer to that question would find him, and he was good with that.

What's next? He planned to stay in Bethany that night and, maybe spend some time with Matthias, if he was there. Then, in the morning, he would make his way into Jerusalem, avoiding the crowds, and meet with those who were part of The Way. He knew that he needed to be careful, he would be an unwelcome visitor in the middle of Passover celebrations. But that was his plan.

By midday, Shimon came to a level stretch and had started to mount his horse, when he saw what appeared to be a body of a dead man, laying by the side of the road. He paused, not getting too close, looked carefully to determine if the man was alive. When he heard him groan, he stepped closer, and examined the body. The man was barely alive. He was nearly naked, had been badly beaten, and was bleeding from multiple wounds to his head, his shoulder, and an arm.

His first impulse was to edge to the other side of the road, and pass by, get on with his journey. Then a thought, a clear remembrance. *Jesus, teaching, there on that hillside. He said many things that sounded right, but one he had a hard time understanding. He said, "Love your enemies and do good to those who hate you."* He remembered thinking *Oh, that would be hard! Jesus told a story that asked the question, 'When did we see you thirsty or injured?' Yes, that was it, and then those words of Jesus, "Go and do likewise"! Huh, what does that mean to me?*

Shimon looked at the man lying there at the edge of the road, and thought: *What if that was me laying there in the dirt and stones of this road, in need of help?* At that moment, Shimon knew in his heart what he had to do. Still, he struggled. He thought, *if I deal with this man, it will surely delay my getting to Bethany.* Yet, he could hear the words of Jesus, there at Gadara, show compassion toward this man, toward this neighbor. He heard his own voice asking, "who is my neighbor?" That was the parable that Jesus told, and Shimon had posed the same question to himself. Then, he said out loud, in reply, 'This man, laying here, before me, he is my neighbor.'

Alone, how can I treat those wounds? He remembered the skin of wine and the last of the expensive silk cloth, packed in the bag strapped to his saddle. Then, he knelt beside the man, proceeded to clean the man's wounds as best he could, pouring on wine, and, without another thought, wrapped them with the costly silk.

He found he was talking to himself as he worked on the man. But then the realization struck him and caused him to smile: he was simply repeating what he had heard from that man, that man of God, Jesus, the Messiah.

When he knew that there was nothing more, he could do for him, here on the road, he made a decision, one that would change him and others. *This man is bigger than I am. I can't lift him onto my horse alone, and I certainly couldn't carry him. What do I do?*

He looked down the road. Where are all those pilgrims that were traveling to Jerusalem? There should be people all around. Where are they? Just then a small group came into view, coming up the hill toward him, a family with small children. They had their hands full. As they approached, he realized that there was another man, alone, behind them, traveling this road by himself, or with that group? An ordinary looking man, no different from me, except younger. As the group passed him, the man stepped over, and, without a word, gestured toward the injured man, and together, they easily lifted him onto the horse.

Quickly, Shimon secured the man to the horse, then turned to thank the one that had helped, but he had already left and was nowhere in sight. Shimon stood there wondering, who was that man? He didn't say a word. He didn't need to, yet there was something about him that seemed familiar.

Chapter 27
BUT GOD…

The merchant was now on foot, leading his horse, with the injured man bound on the saddle, up the steep, rocky grade. It had been slow going and the numbers of Jewish pilgrims travelling to Jerusalem had increased. They would pass him, nod, and looked with curiosity at his horse and burden. Only one family had inquired if he needed any assistance. He thanked them and declined.

He watched the group continue, thinking with the numbers of pilgrims on the road, no robber will risk an attack. He seemed to remember that there was an inn closer to Bethany, or maybe that was just a hope. If there was an inn, it is possible that they would have the supplies he needs to complete treating this man, then leave him in the care of the innkeeper. That stableman in Jericho was correct, it had been three years since he was last on this road. I hope there is still an inn.

He paused on a level stretch, stroking his horse's muzzle and offering some encouraging words, then he turned and continued the slow progress up the hill. Strange thoughts came to his mind, thoughts that were either distracting or comforting, he wasn't sure. The conversation with Matthias had completely recast the "what if's" that had plagued him since Gadara. The disciple had referred to Jesus as 'my master' or 'Man of God', not carpenter or rabbi.

Matthias had also said that most, if not all, of the stories were true, and he had been a witness. Shimon realized that he still had a problem with accepting that all those stories were true. Still, the lessons that Jesus taught there in Gadara, were life-affirming and encouraging, yet challenging. *"Love your enemy"* came to mind, and he struggled again to understand how anyone could do that.

He thought about that first story, one he had heard time and time again, changing water into wine. Matthias said he did not witness but he believed those who had. The logic of that was so unbelievable, he thought *no one could do that. Well, maybe God could*, he thought with a smile.

Then a more serious thought, *of course, God could. How about healing a leper? No one could do that, but…God could. What about restoring sight to a blind boy, or walking on the waters of the Sea of Galilee? No one could do those things, except God.*

Wait! In his mind, he was confronted with a reality that he could not ignore. Why did he stop and help this man? Why didn't I just hurry up the road and leave him? That thought finally brought Shimon to a stop. *Am I so slow of mind? Am I missing what that means?* This is me; this isn't a story about someone else. This is my own experience.

Then he recalled what the man from Pella had said, *"There is no doubt he is a man of God and we; we all have been blessed."* A man of God, that is what he said. Now he had the same experience, and he began to understand the man's struggle.

He again checked the injured man and the ties that secured him to the saddle. The bleeding had stopped, at least for now, and his breathing didn't seem as labored. As he looked at the man, the wonder of what he was seeing, repeated. Who was that man that helped him lift this man up on his horse? How fortunate that he came along just when I needed help. Then another thought took his breath away – *I couldn't do that by myself, but God… No, that man was just another pilgrim travelling with that group*. Still, he wasn't convinced.

In his mind, he went through all that had happened. The small family group followed by a lone man. He had thought, *He's such an ordinary looking man, no different from me, except younger*. Yes, that is exactly what he thought. No, there was something more, something familiar. The hillside of Gadara, the rabbi, the holy man. The first time he saw him he said, '*He's such an ordinary looking man, no different from me, except younger*'.

That thought made him stop, as tears ran down his cheeks, and he knelt, there on the road, his mind racing. What conclusions can I make about all of this? All these stories that I have heard from so many different sources, people swearing they are true, and I disbelieved every one of those, until it became personal to me. What conclusion? There can only be one; this carpenter, this rabbi, this Jesus, is what Matthias called him, a man of God. Maybe more than a man of God! What is more than a man of God? That question was so large and impossible to grasp, even unspeakable, but what indeed is more? God.

Chapter 28

NOT AT MY INN!

It was nightfall when Shimon, leading his horse and nearly exhausted, arrived at the Inn. It was a simple stone building, a rustic hostel built into the side of the hill, a small stable on one side, and sleeping rooms on the other. A short stone wall ringed a little courtyard with benches, and a place to tether horses. Candlelight shone through the windows, and he could see shadows of people moving inside.

He had come a long way. The road had been difficult, his feet hurt, and he was tired. But he knew what he must do. He tethered his horse, checked the man who lay across his saddle, relieved to see that he was still breathing. Shimon knew that the man was desperately in need of more help than he had been able to provide. He hoped the Inn had supplies so that he could finish treating the man, then leave him in the care of the Innkeeper. If supplies were not available, he would need to go the remaining miles up to Bethany, acquire the necessary medicine and bandages, then return.

He stepped up to the door, opened it, and started to enter when the Innkeeper, a short, stocky man with a trimmed beard, and a well-worn tunic that reached to his feet, rushed up, saying, "Welcome. My name is Abbas, and I am the Innkeeper…" then he stopped.

"Hey, wait!" He said, holding up his hand and looking up at the taller man. "You're not a pilgrim. You're not Jewish, from the way you're dressed, I can tell. You could be a Samaritan. Who are you?"

"My name is Shimon," he said in a firm, but calm voice, looking directly at the Abbas. "I am a traveling merchant, and I have just come from Jericho. I don't want a room. I don't plan to stay. I have a man outside who has been assaulted and is badly injured. I treated him as best I could with what I had, but he needs ointments and bandages, and I need olive oil to prepare a poultice for one of his wounds. Do you have those supplies? I would gladly purchase them. Can you help me?"

Abbas, continued to block the way into the Inn. "You didn't answer me," he continued, an aggressive tone in his voice. "I think you are one of those people; Samaritans. I don't want your kind here. This is a respectable establishment and I have a reputation to maintain. I'm not giving or selling you anything and I don't care who is out there. I want you out of my Inn and on your way! Now, don't give me any trouble."

Shimon stepped closer to the Innkeeper and, looking down on the shorter man, spoke in a firm, hard voice; "Listen to me. There is a man out there on my horse, who was beaten and robbed. He is in bad shape. He can't travel further. Do you understand what I am saying? If you don't have the supplies and the bandages I need, alright, but, we, you, and I, need to put him on a bed, here and now. Is that clear? Do you have any oil and cloths for bandages?"

"No, I don't. And even if I did…"

Shimon continued, "Because, if you don't, I will leave the man here, with you, while I go to Bethany to get the supplies needed. I can make that journey, and return here by tomorrow night, or no later than the next morning. I know what I am doing to help this man and I know he will not survive traveling to Bethany.

"So, Abbas," Shimon continued to speak firmly. "I must leave him in your care, until I get back. I will pay you to take care of him until then."

"You still didn't answer me. Are you a Samaritan? Is the man you are helping, a Samaritan? Wait a minute. Did you say you would pay me? How much?"

Shimon sighed in frustration, then said, "As I told you, I am a merchant, and, yes, I am from Samaria. If you want to call me a Samaritan, fine, if it makes any difference. As for the injured man, I don't know who he is. Now, will you help me, help him? Just take care of him long enough for me to get to Bethany and back."

"I asked you how much you would pay? That's a lot of responsibility. I'll have my niece watch over him and see that he gets some water and food if he can eat. But, frankly, I don't even care what happens to him," said the innkeeper. "If he is a Samaritan, I will want him out of here as soon as possible."

."Alright, I will pay you two denarii now, and if you spend more than that I will see that you are repaid. Now, please, help me get him off my horse and into a bed. Then, I will need water and some cloths."

"You know that if he is a Samaritan, this could ruin my business," Abbas grumbled.

Shimon spoke slowly, with controlled anger in his voice, "I told you; I don't know who this man is, I only know that he was attacked and is badly injured. Whoever attacked him, took most of his clothes and any valuables that he may have been carrying. So, I don't know if he's a Samaritan, and, frankly, it doesn't matter, he's a man who needed help and I am doing all I can to provide it. Now, are you going to help, or not?"

"Alright, don't get upset. I don't like this one bit, and two denarii is not enough. Make it three."

"Alright," Shimon said with mounting frustration, "three denarii, is your price. Now we must get him into a bed!"

."I have a storage room at the back. There is a cot there we can put him on. I'm not using one of my fine rooms for this stranger."

Outside, the man, wrapped in Shimon's coat, was draped across the saddle of the horse. He seemed unconscious, but most of the bleeding had stopped. Together, and with some effort, Shimon and Abbas lifted the man from the saddle and carried him into the Inn, to the back room, laying him on a small cot. The injured man moaned, but, remained unconscious.

The Innkeeper commented, "That is a big man! How did you manage to lift him onto the horse?"

Shimon ignored the question, as he looked around the room, then said, "I'll need warm water and some cloths to bath his wounds before I leave."

It was a storage room, indeed. The floor, dirt, the walls lined with shelving, holding supplies for the inn. The cot that held the man was along one wall, and, at the back, a small window.

"I'll have my niece, Mara, bring a basin of water and cloths, as well as blankets. If you want, she can help you, but that will cost you extra."

Shimon simply nodded and turned to the man on the cot, as the innkeeper left.

Chapter 29

DOING LIKEWISE

A few minutes later, a young woman, slender, with long dark hair, wearing an apron over her long dress, entered the room carrying a small jar of oil, a basin of warm water, cloths, and a blanket.

"Oh, my, he really has been hurt," she said. "My name is Mara. Here, let me help you with this," as she set the basin and cloths down, and handed him the oil. Then she covered the man with the blanket, took a cloth, folded it and placed it under the man's head.

"That's good, Mara. I'll check each of his wounds and wash them. You clean his face and see if there are any wounds to his head.

"Your name is Mara? Mine is Shimon," Shimon spoke as he started to clean the wounds on the man's shoulders and arm.

"Shimon, is it? That was very kind of you to help him and bring him here." Then she carefully examined the man's head. "You should look at this wound near the back of his head, it looks bad, but I don't think it's bleeding, right now. Here…." as she gently turned the man's head.

"Yes, that does not look good. His hair has matted into the wound and the blood has dried. With a wet cloth, Mara, very gently see if you can soften the dry blood so that the wound can be cleaned. We may need to cut some of the hair around the wound.

"This man must've been laying there for some time. When I came upon him, I thought he was dead. Others may have thought the same, but there was no sign that anyone tried to help."

He paused and watched Mara work on the man's head wound. "Mara, you have a gentle touch, and see, the hair is softening. I am glad you brought oil; we will need it for the poultice. That will aid in the healing. Could you get a small handful of clean dirt, soil from behind the Inn?"

She returned shortly and handed him the dirt with a quizzical look on her face and asked, "You are making a poultice from that soil?"

"Good, clean soil, Mara. Now take a small piece of cloth put it in the warm water. Using oil, I will make a little mud pie. Now, wring out the extra water and we place this little pie on the cloth and apply it directly on that wound. That is a poultice, and it will help with the healing. Now take a strip of cloth and wrap it around so that it stays in place. Good.

"Tell me, Mara, what are you doing here, at this Inn?"

"The innkeeper is my uncle. Abbas mostly means well, but he can be contrary, and I don't like the attitude he has about Samaritans. Don't worry about him. I'll care for this man until you return. Are you really going to Bethany for supplies, to help this man, and then return? That's quite a journey. You must know the man, to make such an effort to help him."

"No, I really don't know him, and, yes, I need to go. This man needs those supplies. It will take at least a full day and a half, maybe two, but I will return with enough supplies to help this man and for the inn to have a supply on hand, just in case there are others later."

"Why would you do that? We've had other travelers here who have told us about victims of robbery they saw along this road. You know that this road is dangerous, and not just because it's rough and steep, but it seems to attract some pretty mean characters. You're the first person that I've ever heard of helping a victim. If you don't know him, why are you doing this?"

Shimon paused and thought, *why am I doing this? Yes, it's the right thing to do, but why am I? What do I tell Mara? What do I tell myself?* After a moment, he said, "My dear, the answer to that question is complicated, and I'm not sure I have an answer, yet. Until very recently, I might have walked around the man and continued on my way. That would've been the easy thing for me to do. But it seems that is not who I am, now."

"That sounds like something happened to you to make such a change. Is that true? Did something happen, something special, unexpected?" Mara said as she finished taking care of a small wound, covering it with a clean cloth.

"I'm sorry. I'm prying. But Shimon this is a big effort you are making. You said that before you would have passed by, but you may have saved this man's life. That is quite a change. It is more than the effort. Knowing my uncle, this is costing you some. What can you tell me? Oh, dear, I'm asking too many questions."

Shimon simply smiled at her protest, "Mara, I don't mind your asking, for I have some of those same questions. I am still not sure how to explain the change, except that it is new and fresh and complicated. Furthermore, I'm beginning to realize that I have gradually been going through a change of heart over several months. When I return from Bethany, if you're still interested, and I understand it enough to explain, I will share it with you. For now, let me simply say that I met a godly man in a most unexpected time and place. He spoke of love and compassion for others and did some amazing things, and that experience has changed me in the way I look at myself and how I see others. I think that it has given me peace and a calmness to my life. It's very new, Mara, far beyond anything I had ever felt. I will be most happy to share the whole story with you when I return.

"But now, I must be going. This man needs the supplies I'll get in Bethany. If you would check on him, occasionally, and continue to look after the head wound. When the poultice is dry, carefully remove it, gently wash the wound with warm water and put on a little oil and nothing else. If he is conscious and asks for water, give him just a little. It is better for him to sip, frequently, then to take an amount that might cause him to cough. The injuries to his shoulder and arm should be alright until I get back. I don't think he should be up, but if he does, watch that he doesn't fall. I'll return as soon as I can."

"But, Shimon, it's dark and the road is dangerous. Shouldn't you wait until morning?"

"No, Mara. This man is badly injured, especially that head wound, and he needs medicine. What I remember of this section of the road, it is not terribly steep from here to Bethany. I have a torch with me, should I need it, and a good strong horse. I'll be fine."

Shimon thanked Mara for all her good help on what must be done, then thanked her for her help. Then he left the room and looked for Abbas but did not find him. Anxious to get on to Bethany, he walked out of the Inn, approached his horse, stroked its muzzle, said a few words, and untied the reins. It had already gotten dark, so he lit his torch from those burning at the entrance to the Inn, then, leading his horse, he started walking up the road toward Bethany.

He did not notice Abbas step out of the Inn and stood watching him, until he was out of sight. Then he extinguished the torches that lighted the entrance, returned to the Inn, closed, and locked the front door, securely, for the night.

Chapter 30

TO TRUST OR NOT

"We will never see him again," Abbas said, coming into the room where Mara was gathering the soiled cloths. "You can never trust a Samaritan, Mara, you should know that. They lie, they steal, they simply can't be trusted. I tell you again, you will never see that man. Mark my words."

"Uncle, that's not fair! You don't know that about Samaritans, that's just what other people have said."

"Never you mind. Just remember what I'm telling you, he's off to Bethany and then on to who knows where. One thing is certain, he will not return to this Inn."

"I don't agree with you. There was something special about Shimon. Not only did he go out of his way to help, but he also seemed to care about the injured man. I believe that he will be back, just as he promised.

"You know, Uncle, Shimon told me about meeting a godly man, one who spoke of love and peace. He said he really liked what he had heard, and it was changing some of his ideas. I don't know what he was like before, but the person I saw here, caring for this man, treating his wounds, was a person who had compassion. I'll be disappointed if he doesn't return. I want to hear the rest of his story."

"What story? Some fairytales? Mara, be careful. Regardless of what you say that man is a Samaritan, and they are dangerous. I don't like having a Samaritan hanging around, and I'll not have one staying at my Inn. You best take care because they are evil. Besides, we'll never see him again."

"Uncle, I wish you wouldn't talk like that. You really don't know anything about Shimon.

"You asked me about his story, Uncle. I don't know what it is. He just told me about meeting a Godly man and it caused something important to happen to him. Changing him from someone who didn't care about others, to the person we saw. He said if I was still interested, when he returns, he would share his story with me. You might listen in to what he has to say. You might learn something." Mara said as she returned to her work.

"What? Listen to a Samaritan? Never," Abbas called after her. "I'll not do that. But you, you be prepared to be disappointed. And don't spend too much time with this injured man, there is much to be done here at the Inn. I don't want you to neglect your duties."

"Uncle, you know I take my duties seriously, but I will care for this man as best I can. Right now, I am going to my room. I will check on the man later tonight, before I go to bed. Good night."

The next day, Mara, after checking on the injured man, resumed her usual duties, welcoming travelers, helping with the preparation, and serving of meals, and cleaning rooms. It was clear that she was a welcoming hostess to all who entered the Inn.

She had concerns about the unconscious man in the storage room. Frequently, she would check on him, examine the injuries, replace the cloths covering the wound on his head, that was still bleeding, slightly. She wondered who he was and what was he doing alone on Jericho Road? Maybe he was, indeed, a Samaritan, she thought with a smile, thinking that would drive her uncle a little mad.

Early in the evening, after Mara had completed her duties in the dining room, she returned to the storage room to check on "her patient", as Shimon had called him. Entering the room, the man spoke for the first time, a few slurred words, then he motioned toward the water cup. After Mara had helped him sip water, he drifted back to sleep. She noted that his wounds were no longer bleeding, and, before retiring for the night, she saw that he seemed to be resting more peacefully. *Perhaps a good night's sleep would do wonders for his healing*, she thought.

On the morning of the second day, the man was awake and seemed to be improving. Mara helped him sit up and he was able to take a bit of food and some water. His speech was still slurred but he was able to let her know that he still had pain. He spent most of the day dozing, off and on.

Throughout the afternoon and into the evening, Mara would occasionally step outside and sit on a bench. She would look up the road, in the direction of Bethany, in hopes of seeing Shimon returning. She was getting worried that her uncle might be right, that she would not see the Samaritan again.

Near dusk, she and Abbas sat together, relaxing and enjoying the evening air. Her uncle turned to her, "Are you still hoping to see that Samaritan again? My dear niece, I hope you are not disappointed, but didn't he say he would return tonight? I warned you that this might happen. You know I believe you can't trust a Samaritan."

"Uncle, please! He has been gone just two days. He said it might take a little longer. I believe he will be here tomorrow, and you will have to reconsider those thoughts you have about Samaritans."

"Ah, Mara, my dear, I doubt it. But if he comes down this road, and returns to the Inn," Abbas said, pointing, "I'll eat my words!"

"All right, uncle. I don't know how you would do that, but I'll enjoy watching you eat your words!" Mara said with a laugh.

"For now, it is time for me to check on the patient, one last time, then head to my room and prepare for the night. It has been a busy day. As you know we have three quests, so I will be preparing breakfast in the morning. Good night, uncle, dear."

Chapter 31

YOSEF'S STORY

Yosef lay on the small cot, eyes closed. Throughout the day he would drift in and out of sleep. He had some pain, but it seemed to be getting better. His mind was occasionally clear, but foggy, reeling with thoughts, jumbled thoughts, disjointed thoughts that did not make sense. He thought about a Samaritan, of all people. *Why would he think about those awful people?* Then he recalled the sensation of riding a horse, not riding, but being carried on a horse. *Where had that come from?*

The pain again, and then blessed sleep. Much later he awoke, feeling someone placing a cool cloth on his head. That felt good and his headache seemed to be better. He knew he had injuries, pain in his shoulder and arm. A bit of memory came to him. He had been attacked. Why? He was on an errand. What was it? He'd been attacked and robbed. When? Where? Oh, on that road down to Jericho. The feeling of dirt and stones on his face. He was on the ground. *How long had he lain there on the road? When did that happen? How long had it been since the attack? It wasn't yesterday.* He couldn't think. He didn't know.

Then a man came along, a hated Samaritan? No, that's not right. Why did I think that? I have no reason to hate this one, he saved my life. Who was that man, was it a Samaritan who had come into his life? Again, that same thought. Who did rescue me and brought me to this place? What is this place? There was a girl. She put cool cloths on my head. Who is she?

I can't think. My head hurts. Wounds? Where is my tunic? Why am I on this cot? I keep drifting and can't think clearly. Little bits of memory come and go. I was on the road to Jericho. Yes, I remember more. They surprised me and beat me. They took the Temple Tax. More than that, this man, who saved my life, had treated my injuries! He must have brought me to this place, what was this place? How did he get me here? I just can't think straight.

The girl. Mara! That was her name. What an awful name for a gentle angel. Her name should be Angelica, for angel, not Mara. She was far from bitter. My thoughts are everywhere. Whatever her name is, she told me the Samaritan's name, what was it? Why do I keep thinking Samaritan? Ah, yes, Shimon, that was it. He had gone for supplies for me, to treat my wounds. All the way to Bethany or maybe Jerusalem. A Samaritan in Jerusalem? I don't think so, besides, why would he do that?

Yosef slept fitfully. When he awoke, he tried to remember more about what had happened to him. For some reason, he recalled conversations around him, all mixed in with, arguments, that had raged in the Sanhedrin over a mad rabbi. Mara and Shimon talking right next to him. What had they said. Whatever made me think it had to do with his being attacked or, for that matter, why he was on his way to Jericho?

How long have I been here? He could not seem to keep one thought in his mind for any time. Again, he drifted off to sleep.

Chapter 32
SHIMON RETURNS

Just before mid-day, nearly three days after Shimon had left the Inn, he returned, carrying a satchel of bandages, ointments, and other supplies.

Abbas shook his head in disbelief as the Samaritan entered the Inn, and said to him, "I brought extra supplies for your Inn. You never know when injuries will come along."

Abbas, still surprised, accepted the medical supplies without a word of thank you.

"Shimon, I'm so glad to see you," Mara said, walking up to him. "I knew you would be back. My uncle wasn't so sure."

"Mara, you are here. Good. I was a bit delayed on my return. Do you remember I told you I encountered a godly man on my travels, that caused me to wonder about some things? Well, I met one of his disciples, Matthias, in Jericho and shared some of my recent experiences. When we parted, he was on his way to Bethany and Jerusalem. I wasn't sure I would see him again. But, when I stopped in Bethany to get these supplies, I ran into him. He was very upset and told me there were demonstrations and acts of violence going on in Jerusalem. There were even threats against his master, Jesus, as well as some of the disciples, and, yet his master continued to teach in the Temple.

"He told me that Jesus and his disciples and others, were going to gather in a safe house, and he needed to join them. Matthias was most concerned for the safety of his master, and I am worried for the safety of my new friend.

"Mara, you should let Abbas know about what is happening in Jerusalem. Some of that violence could spill down the road near this inn, and you two should be prepared to protect yourselves and secure the Inn."

Shimon nodded toward the storage room and asked, "So, how is our patient?"

"'Our patient' has been showing some improvement. He ate a little food this morning and has been drinking more water. He hasn't tried to stand, yet, although I think he is interested in getting off the cot for a while."

They walked into the room, together, and Shimon quietly said, "Looks like you have been taking good care of him. Has he spoken?"

"He said a few words," Mara whispered, "and there were times when he was mumbling to himself, but it has been difficult for him to speak, and I couldn't always understand what he was saying. He did ask for water, and then seemed to become a little more active when he took bread and a bite of smoked fish. You have the supplies you needed; how can I help?"

"Well, let me see how he is doing." Shimon turned to the man on the cot, whose eyes were open and who seemed to be waking up. "Shalom. My name is Shimon. Can you tell us your name? Do you remember what happened to you?"

The injured man spoke with some difficulty, "My name this Yosef. I don't remember all that happened. I was trying to recall. I know I was robbed and, apparently, I was beaten. I still have some pain." He gestured to his head and side.

"Well Yosef, three days ago, I found you unconscious beside the road. Yes, I agree, you were beaten, and badly, but I don't think any bones were broken. I assumed that you were attacked and robbed. You were dressed only in your under-clothes. You were in bad shape. I brought you to this inn and did the best I could to treat your wounds. Do you have any idea who attacked you?"

Yosef simply shook his head, no.

"Well, this young woman here is Mara. She has been caring for you, while I went to Bethany to get what was needed to properly treat your injuries. Now, I'd like to put ointment and fresh dressings on your wounds. Would that be all right?"

The man nodded,

"So, now, you just relax, Yosef, and let us look to your wounds. We will need to clean them, and then apply ointment. I'm sorry, but this will hurt some."

Shimon and Mara proceeded to work on his wounds gently removing the bloodied cloths that covered the injuries and carefully washing each with a vinegar solution, which caused Yosef to groan in pain.

"Now, Yosef, I'm going to apply some salve, which will help with the pain and the healing, then we will bandage each wound. When we are finished, and after you have rested, let's see if you can stand."

Mara and Shimon worked together to finish treating the man, cleansing the wounds, and applying fresh bandages. After that, they left him to rest for a time.

In the dining room, Mara got some food for Shimon, and told him how grateful she was that he had returned.

"Mara, I am seriously concerned about what is happening in Jerusalem. All that unrest, and during the Jewish celebration of Passover. That is supposed to be a joyous time. When Passover ends, in a day or two, there will be lots of pilgrims on this road. That could mean trouble."

Mara nodded in agreement.

Shimon continued, "I'll be returning home soon, depending on how Yosef is doing. I'd like to avoid Jerusalem, but returning to Jericho is the long way home, and going down this road is not easy. But that is a worry of mine for later."

Shimon realized he was hungry and gave his full attention to the food Mara had given him. Then, later, their conversation resumed.

"Well, my dear, I'm not surprised that your uncle might have had some doubts about my return," Shimon said with a twinkle in his eye, "But I suspect that you were more confident that I would come back. You had asked me what had happened that caused a change in my attitude. I promised that I would answer when I returned, if you are still interested."

"Of course, I'm still interested, and I want to hear the whole story. But I would like my uncle to hear it, as well. I don't know if he will, he has such a negative attitude about people from Samaria, but I will try to convince him."

"I noticed that" Shimon said with a smile. "All right let's wait until your uncle is here. I don't know if Yosef would be interested, but we will ask him. For now, let's see if he is awake and can stand."

They walked into the room and saw that Yosef was alert. "What do you think, Yosef? Are you feeling better? Shall we see if you can stand?"

"Yes, I do feel better, not so much pain. I think it would be good to get up and off this cot, if only for a little while. I'll need some help getting to the room outside, but I'd like to try."

"Excellent," Shimon said with a knowing smile.

Shimon and Mara, stood on either side of Yosef and being careful with his injuries, assisted him to his feet. He stood and took tentative steps. He said, "I'm surprised how weak I am." After a few steps, he said, I think with help I can walk there."

Once seated, Yosef continued with some difficulty, "It is slowly coming back to me. I was on my way from the temple in Jerusalem, where I have responsibilities. I was carrying financial support for the synagogue at Jericho for the days of the Passover celebration. That was the silver they took. I saw only two men, but I think there must have been more. They surprised me. They came on fast, attacked me from behind, then knocked me down. The last thing I can remember was being hit on my head, maybe more than once.

After that, nothing, except waking up on this cot and seeing you, young lady, when you washed my face. And you, Shimon, I am grateful to you. You saved my life. If you hadn't come along…" Yosef choked as he spoke, and tears formed.

"Yosef don't worry about that. I did come along, and you have survived, and you will heal, and be strong, again," Shimon said.

Mara, standing off to the side, seemed to be trying to decide something. Finally, she spoke, "Yosef, I don't know if I should say anything, but I find this interesting. You say that you are one of those in charge of the temple in Jerusalem?"

"Yes, my dear, I am a Sadducee, and a member of the Sanhedrin. We are responsible for maintaining the temple. As you may know, we take our duties seriously."

"Well," Mara, still hesitated, and then, continued. "Ah, Yosef, do you know who Shimon is? He is the one who saved your life and who travelled to Bethany to get supplies for you? Did you know that? He is the one that has been treating your wounds?"

"Yes, I'm aware of that, Mara."

Shimon interrupted, "Yosef, what Mara is having a difficult time explaining, is that I am a merchant from Samaria…"

"What!" Yosef said in a loud voice, a shocked look on his face, "You? You are a Samaritan? You touched me, cleansed, and bound my wounds. You saved my life. You brought me here, on your horse. That's why I had thoughts or feelings about riding on a horse and the thought of a Samaritan kept coming to me."

He paused, took a deep breath then continued, "Why would you do all that? We have hated your kind. We have always considered Samaritans, untouchables! We have despised you. We say that we can never trust a Samaritan. In our community, you are simply not welcome! And you, you Samaritans have done the same to us Jews. You have hated us.

"Yet, look what have you done. We have mistreated you. Yet you brought me here. We have inflicted violence upon you. Yet, you have rescued me. We have hated your kind. Yet, you travelled for supplies. We cursed you, and now, you have treated my wounds, you have saved my life. Why, Shimon, when we have done so much against you, hurtful things, yet you did this? You did all of this for me? Why?"

"Yosef, the truth is, I don't know. Maybe it is time for this problem we have between our nations to end. Mara asked me the same question when we first settled you here. I promised that I would try to answer her, to explain. Now, if you wish, I will try to answer the question you both have asked. But, please, listen to the whole story. It will take a bit of time to tell, because I am just now trying to understand it, but I think it is important that you hear it all."

"Shimon, this is so unusual," Yosef said, "I should like to hear what you have to say. I'll try to stay alert."

Mara interrupted, "Shimon, before you start, let me find my uncle. I would like him to hear what you have to say."

Chapter 33
THE STORY CONTINUES

Yosef lay propped up on the cot, while Mara and Abbas sat in chairs. All waiting for Shimon to continue sharing his life-changing experience. Each one caught up in their own life experiences and biases.

Shimon continued, "I want to tell you about my time in Scythopolis. I always enjoyed that luxurious city, with its beautiful inn and large marketplace. I stayed three days, and it was in the dining room of the Inn that I heard some of these same stories told by others, except many referred to the man as 'a man of God'. I wanted to argue with them, telling them that such stories weren't true, but, by then, my heart wasn't in it. I was beginning to doubt what I believed about the stories.

"I was about to offer my opinion, when somethings were said that caused me to reexamine the conflict I was experiencing. First, a man spoke up, telling us that a relative of his, a priest, was at the wedding where the man, this rabbi you speak of, turned water into wine. He was convinced that it was true. This from a priest, who was there! That got my attention!

"I was still grappling with my doubts, when, shortly after that, still another man complicated my thinking. This man was a merchant from Pella, in Syria, and he told of attending a gathering near Bethsaida, up north, and listening to a holy man from Galilee. That merchant spoke of the power of this man's teaching, but he said the most amazing event was when that man fed the crowd! He told us he watched the holy man take a small amount of food, blessed it and baskets appeared! He told us there were thousands of people on that hillside and called it a miracle.

That man was really shaken, crying, shedding tears. He could barely get through telling us about it. His experience touched all of us deeply. Let me tell you, this was no story for that man, he was a witness.

"I still had my doubts, even though it was obvious to me that this man was greatly affected by his experience. I looked around the dining room and everyone seemed intent on what the merchant was saying.

"I thought again of stories, events that took place and the people who were there. It seemed strange to me that in the telling of these stories, it was with conviction and that the man behind each of the stories was the same one, this rabbi from Nazareth.

"Remember, this has been my experience in just these past several days, and I'm still trying to understand. Now I must tell you what happened to me, just three days after my experience in Scythopolis. Two powerful things, miraculous things. I was on my way to the market town of Gadara, just east of the Jordan. On the hillside, outside of town, I sat at the edge of a large crowd and listened to a holy man. I was surprised to learn that he was Jesus of Nazareth. I stayed all afternoon, listening to his teaching about love and giving lives meaning and purpose. What a powerful experience that was.

"But then, a miracle! Just like the man from Pella had said, Jesus, fed us! I'm telling you; he fed us all bread and fish! All of us, thousands! He took a small amount of food, a boy's lunch, blessed it and baskets of the food were passed around. I took fish and bread, and before I passed the basket on, I saw that the basket was still full. Oh, I tried to explain it, to figure out how he could've done that trick, but there was no trick, it was a miracle and I had to accept it as fact."

Shimon paused, looked around the room. Yosef seemed deep in thought, while Mara was mesmerized. Abbas sat quietly, a doubtful look on his face.

"You said this was Jesus of Nazareth?" Yosef asked, almost in a whisper. "I have heard him speak and what he said had power," but then he lapsed into silence again.

Shimon stood, looked at Yosef for a long moment, then paused to examine the wounds on his head. The bandages were still clean. Satisfied, he then continued.

"That experience wasn't something that another told me, it was something I had seen and experienced. This was different, this was powerful, this was persuasive. Yet, accepting it was another thing. I spent the next two days visiting vineyards trying to erase the thoughts of what I had experienced, before I traveled on to Jericho.

"My experience in Gadara was real and removed most of my doubt. When I stabled my animals in Jericho, I met the stable manager. He told me of a joyous family event that happened just a few days before I arrived. He said that a holy man, the one they called Jesus stopped where his son, born blind, was begging, and this Jesus restored his sight! That's right, another story told to me. Another miracle?"

At that, Abbas stood and said, "These stories are just that, stories. I don't believe in miracles, or a storyteller they called a man of God. I know that stable manager, Timaeus. His son is Bartimaeus, and he is blind. Timaeus has stopped here before. You say his son can now, see? That would be a blessing for the whole family if it happened. Did you talk to the son?"

"No, his father said he followed Jesus up the road to Bethany. With his new sight, he became a follower of Jesus."

"I would have guessed," Abbas said with a accusatory tone, "just another story from a Samaritan!", as he started to leave the room.

"Uncle, stop that!" Mara said, which caused Abbas to turn, looked at Mara, then continued out the room.

Shimon ignored what had been said, and continued, "Mara, I told you earlier about meeting a disciple of Jesus, first in Jericho, then again in Bethany. His name is Matthias, and he had been with Jesus for more than two years. He is the one that confirmed many of the stories that I had heard. We talked well into the night, and in the morning, Matthias left for Jerusalem where he joined his master and the other disciples. Now, I am worried about him for he told me about riots in Jerusalem."

Yosef immediately raised his hand and said, "Wait. What riots? What's happening in Jerusalem? Tell me!"

"Matthias told me there is great tension in the city, and there had been riots between the followers of Jesus and the Jewish leadership. I didn't fully understand what he was saying, but it was clear that he was very worried, especially for his Master, and the continuing danger in the city.

"Yosef, from your role in the temple, do you know anything about this?"

"All I know is that when I left the temple there was growing concern about the popularity of this Jesus. I was under the impression that the decision by the Sanhedrin was not to do anything that would upset the people, especially during Passover week. I started for Jericho three days before Passover so what you learned from your friend is news."

"Yes, Yosef, disturbing news. I wonder, if this Jesus is just a good teacher, why is there such unrest and threats in Jerusalem against him? I am beginning to believe he is not just a good teacher.

"Let me tell you about one more thing. When I came upon Yosef lying there in the road, I did not debate, I did not struggle, I knew what I had to do. In my mind, I heard the words of Jesus telling me to help the man and I did. Yosef, you can thank me all you want for saving your life, but it wasn't me, it was this holy man, it was this Jesus of Nazareth. I was simply his hands.

"So, yes, it is disturbing that there is such opposition to Jesus, a holy man of God."

Yosef lay on the cot, looking at Shimon in a thoughtful way, but remained silent.

Mara was silent for a short time, before she said, "I don't know how much of your story my uncle heard. I'll ask later. But, Shimon, I need to think about all that you have told us. All those stories, those events, that apparently had such an effect on you, have meaning for us, as well.

"I was wondering. You said that this Jesus left Jericho for Bethany, several days before you got there. He would have come by the Inn. I wonder how I missed him. I would have liked to meet him, this man of God."

"Mara, what Matthias told me caused the disciples great worry. That was more than three days ago. I believe that Passover will be over soon. Hopefully, there will be calmness again in the city. Still, we will await more information."

Shimon turned to Yosef, who seemed to have fallen asleep on the cot. "We should let him rest. We can talk more later today. For now, I think I'll step outside and get some air. Later, I would like to see if Abbas has any questions."

Chapter 34

CONFLICTED

It was several days later when Yosef was wakened by people talking quietly in the next room. He was now in one of the guest rooms, a result of Mara's persuasiveness with her uncle. *Who was talking? Sounds like Mara and Shimon. I must have fallen asleep trying to recall all that the Samaritan had shared. I found some of it hard to believe, not only that, but some were against what I had understood all my life.*

He recalled, not that long ago, when he stood on the fringe of a crowd, listening to the teaching of this rabbi, Jesus, and agreeing with much of it. He had seen some minor points that he had trouble accepting, but no conflicts. What had Nicodemus said? He believed that Jesus' teaching 'seemed unorthodox, too simplistic, or mysterious to truly be followed.' *I didn't agree with some of what he said, except on the absence of conflict and he had said so in his report to the Sanhedrin.*

His memory returned in little pieces and gradually he remembered. Now, Yosef did have a conflict. *I owe my life to a Samaritan! That is hard to accept. But he was not like any Samaritan that I have known. Have I ever really known a Samaritan?* He couldn't remember. *This one was a man that cared, cared for me! He went out of his way to help me. What did he call me? Yes, he called me friend and he called me a neighbor. How could I be a neighbor? Nonsense! Nevertheless…*

This Samaritan had shared experiences that changed him, from a selfish and dishonest merchant, who cared only for himself, into this man who saved my life. What power had allowed him to be able to do that? What had changed him so?

Then, of all things, he quoted the Torah! I suppose a Samaritan could quote the Torah! What part… Yes, "Love the Lord your God with all your heart and with all your soul and with all your strength," and that was correct, right out of the sacred writings. But then he said that it was the first and greatest Commandment, but there was a second one, a Second Commandment.

What was it? He couldn't think. *Love the Lord your God… Oh, why can't I remember? It was something that didn't make sense, yet somehow it belonged. What was it? Love the Lord your God was the first and greatest Commandment and the second was like it… Like it? How could it be like it?*

He had called me "neighbor', could that be it? No, I'm not a neighbor. Yet, it was 'neighbor', that was it. The Second Commandment was "Love your neighbor as yourself." That's not in the Torah, but it sounded right, it sounded like it should be.

As Yosef recalled these things, tears came to his eyes, and he felt the rightness of it. It belonged. *Love the Lord and love your neighbor as you love yourself. That was when he called me friend! He told me I was his neighbor.*

What had changed Shimon from a dishonest merchant who did not care for others, to the man that reached out and saved my life? Does that mean I'm indebted to him? If it weren't for him, I would not be here. If it weren't for him, I would not have this conflict that is causing me so much distress. Yet, why am I conflicted? Is it so hard to face the possibilities that I must change?

He replayed in his mind, all the discussion in the Sanhedrin. *It seemed to me that too many of my brothers wanted to do away with this rabbi. I had listened to him not only in Jerusalem, but I traveled into the countryside of Judea to hear him. Yes, he said a few things contrary to Mosaic Law, but he simply wasn't a threat. I was not happy during those discussions, and thought, there must be a different way. But was there? Did those protests in Jerusalem have anything to do with this rabbi?* he wondered.

His mind returned to the question, *who was this Jesus of Nazareth? Was he a miracle-worker or trickster? If he was a miracle-worker, could he be The Messiah?* Yosef closed his eyes and let his mind drift to what he had been taught about the signs announcing the coming of The Messiah. *Yes, in the Holy Scrolls, it speaks of miraculous works and there is a refer-*

ence to raising from the dead, the resurrection. Furthermore, in the Ketubot Ceremonial Vows there is mention of the resurrection of the dead.

I should go back and study the Torah. Shimon had spoken of his growing belief in Jesus. Belief that this man was a holy man, who did miracles, and maybe he had heard talk that this man could be The Messiah. How could that be? How would a Samaritan even know about The Messiah, let alone, believe it? Did he believe it or had he heard others saying that. But this man could not be The Messiah, he is alive. There had been no resurrection!

He had been pondering those thoughts all afternoon, thoughts which seemed to conflict with what Shimon had been taking about. *I remember hearing some of those same stories of the rabbi's ministry and never considered that they were true. But now, after what Shimon has described, how can I deny them?*

In the midst of that thought, Mara entered the room, asking, "How are you feeling, Yosef? Would you like some water, a bit of food?"

Yosef said, "A little water would be good. Food? Maybe later. Then, for a while, I'll close my eyes and rest. I have much to think about."

"Resting would be good," Mara said as she helped him to some water. "I'll come back later to check your injuries. I believe Shimon has done a good job. That bed probably feels better than that old cot in the storage room."

"Oh, yes, this is a nice room, this bed does feel good."

Chapter 35

THE CRUCIFIXION

He didn't know how long he slept but he was awakened by loud and excited talking in the lobby. He could hear Abbas speaking above the voices of the others. He heard words like *"execution"* and *"radical rabbi"* and *"riots in the street"*. What was happening?

He called out to those in the lobby and Shimon came in. He had a sad look on his face. He sat down in the chair next to the bed and quietly told Yosef, "They have executed the rabbi, Jesus. They beat him and then they crucified him, there on Calvary. Why would they do that? He was a holy man; he was a holy man!"

They sat in stunned silence trying to absorb the impact of this news. It had been less than ten days after the miracle on the hillside of Gadara and all that had happened in Jericho. Shimon had hoped to be able to hear him speak again. What turned the crowd against Jesus?

Yosef recalled the attitude of some members of the Sanhedrin after he had given his report. They didn't agree with him, and they continue to call for the stoning of this "trouble-maker rabbi", as they called him. Did they finally get rid of this popular teacher?

Yosef asked Shimon, "You told us about the three visitors that came to your shop and shared with you what happened in their village when this rabbi came to visit, and how it had changed them. It was during that time that Jesus told that woman that he was the Messiah. Was there anything else about that conversation that might help us understand what has happened?"

"No," Shimon replied, "The conversation was brief, and, at the time, I had no reason to raise other questions. It's another one of those times when I wish I had followed through a little better, but the fact is my understanding has changed since then. I am convinced, even if Jesus has indeed been executed, it doesn't change the power of his message.

"Yosef, something happened to me on that road where I found you. I had to have help in getting you onto the saddle, and suddenly help was there, then it was gone. A man came by, helped me and then by the time I turned around he was gone. My first thought was where did he come from? Then for some reason I got to thinking about all the stories, the so-called fables, that had been driving my thinking for months. Stories of healings, miraculous things like calming a storm, raising a little girl for the dead. The thought that overwhelmed me at that moment was that a man could not do those things, but God could.

"Yosef, I don't know a lot, but I know this, God is in all of what we have experienced -- Jesus' teachings, the feeding of the crowds, everything. If God is in this, then this is not the end. I don't know about you, but, my friend, there's more to come."

The two were silent for long moments, then the prophesy of Ezekiel 37:12, that Yosef had memorized as a child, came to mind, and he quoted it aloud: "*So says the Lord God: O my people, I am going to open your graves and bring you up from them; I will bring you back to the land of Israel. Then you, my people, will know that I am the LORD, when I open your graves and bring you up from them And I will put My spirit into you, and you shall live.*'

Yosef continued, "If Jesus is…special, there is indeed more to come. The prophecy of a resurrection is in the Torah. It is included within the Scrolls, in the sacred Word! Now, I wonder why Sadducees do not believe it. Why have I not seen this before? Why have I been blind? Shimon, it is right there in the Amidah! Three times a day I say the prayer, we speak the blessings, yet I did not see it, or understand its meaning. But now…Oh, Lord!

"I know resurrection is a sign, a holy sign. So, this rabbi, this Jesus, that I saw and heard teach, and you have done the same, who was alive and because of that did not fit the prophecy as being The Messiah. Now…" Yosef paused, a prayerful silence of meaning, and bowed his head.

Shimon continued with an idea, almost too big for him to grasp, "Now, Jesus is no longer alive…but I am convinced there is more to come," he said. He rose, tears in his eyes, and quietly left the room.

Chapter 36

BACK IN THE TEMPLE?

More to come. Yosef continued to turn that thought over in his mind. He again considered refreshing his understanding of the prophecy regarding the Messiah, once he is back in the Temple.

Back in the Temple? Ah, there's a question. Could he return to his role in the Temple? Should he? He knew that the resurrection was a sign of the Messiah, yet i*t was contrary to the conservative Sadducees politics and beliefs. However, there were times when I think our community is more concerned about maintaining our power in the present and less interested in issues of the afterlife and God's great concern for the poor and the oppressed. I am finding it harder and harder to endorse that which I have lived for so long. The doubts that I have had, what I heard from Shimon, the death of the rabbi, which caused my own sense of loss, and all the thoughts I have had about the resurrection. What does all that mean? My thinking is changing. Can I even return to the temple with this change of heart? I could be subject to judgment by my community, and I am sure that one or two will raise the matter of blasphemy, which, they will remind me, carries the death penalty.*

Fatigue was catching up with him and his thinking was fuzzy and conflicted. He was unsure what he believed, or how that belief would change his situation, and now that puzzling phrase, more to come... During that thought, he slept.

He didn't know how long he slept, when he was startled awake by Mara returning to the room. "Oh, good, you are awake," she said. "Here, let me look at your injuries, then I will see about getting you some food.

I think your injuries are coming along fine. No more bleeding, and that is a good sign."

"What do you think about what Shimon has told us?" Mara asked as she examined the bandages. "That was an amazing story, one that I not only liked, but I felt something within my being, something exciting. But now, that man, that rabbi is dead. What is going to happen and what does that mean?

Mara continued, "I never thought much about God and how my relationship with God could affect my life, but now I'm wondering. When Shimon talked about his experience on the hillside, seeing a miracle by Jesus, when that crowd was fed, that caused my heart to almost burst inside, and I cried. I don't know what that meant. Now we hear that the rabbi is dead. I'm sad and excited as the same time.

"I'm just talking on and on. Let me get you some food," she said as she left the room.

Yosef had not said a word. He wanted to talk to Deborah, his wife, about this, but, of course, that was out of the question for now. Mara had her own questions and needed to talk. He closed his eyes to concentrate, but his mind kept coming back to matters that were in opposition to Sadducee belief. If only he could talk to someone who might understand his conflict.

Chapter 37

SHARED CONFLICTS

As if an answer to his unspoken wish, Shimon tapped on the door and quietly came in and stood by the bed. "I thought you might be awake. I should let you rest."

"Please stay, I welcome an opportunity to talk further. I sense we are both conflicted, in different ways, but maybe not so far apart. What I've experienced in these days has caused thoughts to flood my mind. How long has it been?"

"It has been more than a week," Shimon said.

"Yes, not very long, and yet long enough to bring some of my confusion out into the open. Maybe I can get your thoughts. My father was a Pharisee, a teacher of the law, and he instructed me, all my life. He did not like it when I became a Sadducee, for he opposed some of their thinking. Over time I realized that I was in conflict with their teaching and what I had learned all my life. And now your experience further complicates things. Does that make sense?"

"Yosef, I can understand why you would have a conflict. I can relate to that kind of confusion. I was raised in a home where there was very little discussion of religion or what we believed. My mother was gone, died when I was a child. I told you my father was a rather inflexible, demanding businessman. I heard all about that life growing up and when he died, I became a businessman at seventeen. One thing he did teach me, was to take advantage of the tension between a Jew and a Samaritan and capitalize on it. In my merchant travels, I tried to act like a Jew, selling to Jews and Greeks. I was the friendliest, most honest person they ever met, never telling I was from Samaria. I took advantage of them. I thought it as just business, but now I see the dishonesty.

"That is probably not very helpful to your situation. I don't believe that not revealing your conflict, would work for you. I think you have a conflict of conscience."

"You are correct, Shimon. My conflict is in what I believe. I can understand how your experience has changed you. In like manner, what you have shared with us has further complicated my thinking. That's not right, not complicated, maybe defined would be a better word. Yes, hearing your story has helped me define my own conflict. Hearing of your experience has clarified my dilemma, and helped me see it as a… dare I say, a blessing?

"What had we said earlier? We talked about the death of the rabbi and the belief that God has more for us to experience. I have to say, Shimon, that thought has caused my mind to spin."

"Can you believe we're having this conversation?" Shimon said, which caused both to chuckle.

Yosef, continued, "In the eyes of some within the Sanhedrin, I would be a candidate for a stoning! See, that is part of my conflict. Before I became a member of the Sanhedrin, I struggled with the beliefs of the Pharisee versus the Sadducee, thinking there must be a way to resolve that. When I was given the assignment within the Sanhedrin to seek out Jesus, and listen to what he had to say, it only added to my struggle because now I was pulled in not two but three different directions."

"That much I can understand, Yosef. But I sense it's more than that. There is a big practical element for you. You have a role within the Temple and that is how you support your family. How will this conflict impact that important part of your life?"

"That's exactly where I struggle, Shimon. I think I'm resolving parts of my belief system, but now I must grapple with the practical aspects of who I am in Jerusalem, and specifically in the Temple, and if that changes, what about my family?"

"I'm not sure I can help you with that one, Yosef. All I can say is that for the first time I have something that I can believe in and on that belief, I'm going to reshape my life. I can tell you about one thing that has been helpful for me, for it helps me sort out my next steps. This may sound strange, but I talk to this Jesus. Can you believe that? I started a few days after my experience in Gadara. Early in the morning, I talk to him as if he is standing right here, telling him what I'm hoping to do. And then I listen. I just listen to what my heart is telling me. There are times I sense a direction and I have tears, tears of joy. That time of talking with Jesus has become important for me.

"Yosef, we talked about Jesus being executed, and just before I came in here, a traveler stopped by saying there was a rumor that Jesus came to life and was seen. The man said that hardly no one believes that, but it is upsetting the Jews and the Romans. He said there was even talk that he was the Messiah. Now there is more violence in Jerusalem."

Yosef said. "A resurrection? Whether I believe that or not, doesn't alter my conflict, but what if he is the Messiah."

"Yosef, if you believed that there has been a resurrection, and he is the Messiah, then it would make a big difference, in both of us. If we believe that Jesus is a man of God, and he did all those things we have heard about and what I witnessed then, then for me, he is still here for you and me."

"Shimon. All my life I have prayed to God three times a day. We have set times and set prayers. I've never thought about talking to God, only about saying the prayers, and praising him. I would find talking to him strange. When I sought Jesus out and listened to what he had to say, I realized that I was not that much older than he. I saw a young man with a special way of speaking. A man of God? Now maybe the Messiah. Hmm, I must think about this some more.

"Shimon, thank you so much, I think what you have shared helps me. Maybe we can talk more later. For now, I feel the need to rest."

Chapter 38

WHAT AM I TO THINK?

Abbas sat outside the Inn, dressed in a brocaded tunic, his beard combed, neatly trimmed, and brushed until it shown. He looked, every inch, the dutiful innkeeper that he was.

It was a beautiful morning, not a cloud in the azure blue sky. The heat of the coming day had not yet set in. The familiar view across the Jordan Valley was illuminated by the brilliance of the early morning sun.

There would be more travelers on the road again today, as the days of Passover were coming to an end. The pilgrims that made the trek to Temple, would be returning, traveling back to Jericho. Traffic on the road was always good for business, especially in the dining room, and during the High Feast Days, Passover, Shavuot, and Sukkot.

He smiled as he thought about the last nine days. What a series of events! So much to think about, thoughts that ran contrary to all that he had believed. He had to ask himself, what did he believe? He was a Jew, but he never considered himself a religious man. He rarely had made pilgrimage to the Temple, for any of the high holy days. *It's been years since I had been there. Maybe at the time of Mara's dedication. Yes, that would have been it. Ten years ago! Ten years! How time passes. That would make her twenty-three, and unmarried! Goodness!*

And then there was the Samaritan. All his life he had been cautioned about them; their dishonesty, their violence against the Jews, and the belief that they cared for nothing but themselves. In the fifteen years that he ran this inn, he had not allowed Samaritans, not to eat, not to stay. Not even to sit on these benches that lined the road.

Then Shimon arrived with the injured Yosef, and for days he had watched a Samaritan help a Sadducee, a member of temple ruling council! *How did that happen?* Just saying that seemed impossible and made absolutely no sense to him, until...he reluctantly listened to what the Samaritan, had said about a changed life, and what had caused him to rescue and treat Yosef, as if he was a neighbor. *A neighbor! That was so confusing! After all I have seen and heard, what was am I to think?*

What was even more confusing, was when Yosef and Shimon talked together about what was happening in Jerusalem. All that trouble, and they both were concerned, and seemed to be in agreement! In agreement! Even with the crucifixion of the rabbi that the Samaritan admired so. The world is turning upside down. How could that be?

After a time, Abbas calmly thought about all that had been said. Shimon, a Samaritan that cared about another person. Would it have made a difference if Shimon had known that the beaten man was a Sadducee? Somehow, he didn't think so. There was something genuine and caring about this man, this Samaritan! Mara had said that much earlier, she saw that. More than that, Abbas felt a kinship to him, like he was a good person, a trusted friend. What a thought! He almost laughed out loud!

Just as suddenly, another picture came to mind, a picture with more details. *Shimon, the Samaritan, who didn't just care, he went out of his way. He had traveled the road to Bethany and back. He used his own money to restock the Inn with medical supplies, without a thought that, somehow, he would be repaid. He never even asked! And I thought we would never see him again, and, yet...* He smiled at the thought that he would eat his own words!

There was something else, a word that Shimon had said. What was it? Likewise. Yes, he said he had to do likewise. What does that mean? Had the Samaritan been beaten and robbed, and been rescued? No, that wasn't the point. What was the point?

As if in answer to his own question, Abbas played out what had happened in his mind. *If the Samaritan had been the one beaten and left for dead, he would want others to help him, to treat him, to save him. So, to go and do likewise, means to, what is that saying from the Torah, he learned as a child?* "Do unto others as you would want them to do to you." *Yes. That is what likewise meant.*

For the longest time Abbas sat, thinking about that unusual idea. *To do likewise. What would have happened if that had been me laying there? Would I want someone to do what Shimon had done for Yosef? Of course. And, it would not have mattered who that person was. No, it would not have mattered.*

Another thought occurred to him: *does 'likewise' have anything to do with all that talk about being a neighbor, seeing others as friends? Yes, of course it does. That is what Shimon was saying.*

"I don't think I can do that," Abbas spoke out loud and it startled him. *I must think about this, it seems too radical and maybe dangerous for this lowly innkeeper, on this isolated stretch of rough road. Treat everyone as a neighbor? Is that reckless? Is it foolishness? Dangerous? Not every Samaritan is good, he thought. But then, not every person is good. What he had seen and experienced here was a good man, a good Samaritan.*

It was then that he remembered where he had seen Yosef before. *It must have been nearly two weeks ago, maybe longer. I was sitting here, early in the morning, when this grandly attired priest, with a finely detailed yarmulke on his head, walked by. He carried a beautifully carved staff and wore a stunning tallit, beautifully embroidered, with glistening prayer tassels.* He recalled, especially, the hand-tooled sandals the priest wore. At the time, he thought, *what a foolish man, travelling alone on this road, this rough and dangerous road. He is just begging to be attacked and robbed. Mara had even commented on it. I think she would remember him.*

Then, even when he helped Shimon lift the injured man from the horse, he did not recognize him as the priest he had seen earlier. *What a time it has been.*

Chapter 39
IT'S GOD'S LOVE

Abbas stood and walked into the Inn. He glanced into the dining room where Mara was clearing tables and taking dishes into the kitchen. He thought that she was such a good worker. *During her years here, she has become an indispensable part of the Inn staff. I think she could manage this Inn on her own.*

The innkeeper looked in the storage room where so much had happened. Mara had already cleaned and straightened the cot and the shelves. He remembered sitting just outside that room, listening to Shimon, unwilling to enter and join the others for fear of suggesting that he wanted to hear what was being said, which he did, of course. Then he had become so interested in what was being said, that he joined them.

He recalled his own argument within his head, telling him, *that is a Samaritan speaking! Do you really believe him? Then another voice telling him that it is not where he is from, but what had happened to him and its effect that mattered. Do I want to believe him? Do I want to believe a Samaritan? Do I want to believe him? Yes, yes, I do,* the innkeeper thought, as tears came to his eyes.

A voice from behind him, "Uncle, what's wrong?"

"Wrong? Nothing's wrong, my dear Mara, nothing, and yet, everything! Have I told you how much I value your role in this Inn of ours? I do, you know.

"Help me understand, my dear, what am I to think? All these many years I have held certain thoughts, and now, in just a few days the ideas that I built this Inn upon and have succeeded, are being challenged.

What am I to think? A Samaritan helping a Sadducee! A Sadducee listening to a Samaritan! The world is upside down! It is quite maddening, and yet it is quite right. Is that crazy?"

"No, uncle, it is not crazy," Mara said gently. "It's God's love. It's the God you and I have worshipped all our lives, giving us a better understanding of love, His kind of love, an all-inclusive kind, that embraces everyone. That is what it means."

"That is the source of my struggle, Mara. You are a smart woman. I want to believe that you are right. I don't know why I struggle with this so much, but you explained it clearly. Thank you. I believe that Shimon has had a real impact on you, too, my dear niece."

Mara remained silent for some time before answering, "What Shimon has said and what happened to him was powerful, not only for him but also for us, you, and me. Now, here we are wondering, maybe even disputing, changes in our thinking. How will it change our lives? I believe this is God working in us. Moving us toward His purpose."

"Mara, do you believe that? We are Jews. What Shimon has told us, requires me to consider so much what happened, right here, before our eyes, in just a short span of time. It's not just the strongly held views of the Sadducee or a Pharisee, or my long-held negative views toward Samaritans, it goes beyond all of that."

"I know, Uncle. I remember what the rabbi told me about you during my time of dedication at the Temple. He said that when you first opened this Inn people thought that this was a perfect place for you, because your strength was in being approachable. He used the term 'hospitable' and thought you would create a place where people would feel welcomed. He said he thought of that when he decided to try convincing me to come and meet you. Then he told me all about that and I have held that in mind ever since. Now I am here, and I do my part to make people feel welcomed. I want others to know that this Inn is, indeed, a good place to visit."

"Yes," Abbas agreed, "I want our reputation to be one of hospitality, but also that we are a safe place to stay on a rough and dangerous road.

"Don't you think it strange that Shimon and Yosef were both on this road at the same time, Mara? I have seen other priests and Levites travelling, usually in pairs or groups, but rarely have I been aware that a Samaritan would travel this road. A Samaritan would have no reason to visit the Great Temple, let alone, travel without a companion. Yet, it happened, and we know what followed."

"Yes, Uncle, we know, and what followed has affected the lives of those two, and ours, as well. I can imagine that this was God's plan. Yet, this rabbi, this man of God has been crucified and I hve to believe there is more to God's plan. Think of it, Uncle, this may change the character and hospitality of this Inn.

"Yosef will face radical changes in his life, that will touch the lives of his family, and probably many others. What will he do? I am worried for him."

"What about you, Mara. Here you are a young woman, with talents you have just begun to explore. And now your faith is being tested. At your age, most women are married and have children."

"Uncle, I have thought about that many times, and about my mother. Being married and having children will follow in time, according to God's time, not mine.

"How will what has happened now affect me? Maybe I am more concerned with making others feel welcome here, but in the years ahead? I have such a soft place in my heart for orphan children, a condition I lived for many years. Will I follow that need to do something? Would I go to Jerusalem or to Capernaum, as Shimon has suggested? Only my Lord knows.

"And Shimon. He has such a potential ministry, sharing his own experience, and the lessons that Jesus taught to those who had never heard the message. An exciting ministry. Will he stay in Samaria? I believe his message of Jesus will spread as he shares it with others. I think that is true for each of us.

"And you, my uncle. How will this time change you? Will it change the nature of this Inn? I don't think so. Will you share this story of

Shimon, with others? And personally, how will his story change you over the coming years?"

"So many questions," Abbas commented and, what he said next, surprised Mara. "But the truth is, we don't need answers, we just need to trust that God's plan for each of us is perfect and fits each one of us. I'm beginning to believe that with my whole heart."

Mara hugged her uncle, saying, "You are one dear man. I am so fortunate to be here and to have your support. I love you."

The two left the storage room, Mara returned to the kitchen to resume her duties, while Abbas continued with his usual routine of preparing the Inn for more visitors.

Chapter 40
TIME TO GO

It was early in the morning when Shimon walked into the dining room after spending time with Yosef. Mara was in the kitchen preparing breakfast for those staying at the Inn.

"Shimon, you are up early this morning. Do you have plans? Surely, you're not leaving us quite yet."

"Ah, Mara, it is time for me to move on. I just talked with Yosef. He is healing quite well and will soon make his own way home. I have plans to meet with some men in Bethany and, maybe, Jerusalem, too. That sounds so strange to my ears, 'meet in Jerusalem.' Who would have thought?

"I want to say something to you, my dear. You have been marvelous. You have a sense of compassion that anyone you meet can recognize. You care for others, and I would guess that you now have another concern, born out of compassion that relates to your roots. You and I have talked about the orphan children, and you have some wonderful ideas, that will bring about a change in their lives in more ways than you know. It's a worthy mission. You may be surprised where support of your ideas may come from over the years. I think our Lord has given you a purpose. A sacred purpose, and I want to encourage you.

"While I am off to Samaria and my own mission, as you call it, I have plans to work with others in sharing the lesson of love. The time may come when our paths will cross, and I will learn how your purpose is being acted out. I will always be supportive of it, you know.

"Now, one more important thing I must say to you. You told me your story, your early years, alone, and you told me that your name is not Mara. You put the name, Mara, on yourself when you were feeling deserted and alone, and thought you had no hope. You are now a young woman with a bright future and have not been that other sad person for a very long time. Naomi is your true name, and it describes a beautiful person, inside and out. It is time for you to reembrace your real name, along with your new purpose. You will always be Naomi in my mind, and I will hold you in my prayers as you go about this new commitment."

Shimon pulled her into a big hug, and "Jesus loves you, my dear, and so do I. Go in peace, God's peace."

With her name restored, she brushed tears from her cheeks, smiled up at Shimon, then turned and walked back into the kitchen, there was work to be done and watching him leave would be too hard.

Shimon walked out of the dining room and stepped to the front door where he saw the innkeeper sitting outside.

"Mind if I join you, Abbas? It has been a very eventful time for us, and I want to thank you for the hospitality that you've extended to Yosef and to me, probably under some difficult circumstances. I know you and I both have a bias that we must recognize and leave in the past. I understand how that attitude, that we share, has evolved. I think we both know how important it is that we move on, because God looks on the inside, and so should we."

"Shimon, I agree. I find it hard for me to say this, but this has been a blessed time of change, all for the better, even though we got off to a bad start. I will still have a certain guardedness should other Samaritans come to the Inn, but I'll try hard to practice what you were describing, to see others as neighbors. Do you know how hard that is for me to consider after a whole lifetime of hating, only to find a better way, through friendship."

"Why Abbas, I do believe that there is a teacher buried somewhere in that heart of yours." And they both laughed at the comment.

"Listen, Shimon. Your telling of your experiences has really touched me in ways that I am not sure I can explain. This Inn has always been my life. Then, along came Mara, a blessing, and both the Inn and the innkeeper began to change. Then I met Lazarus, and he helped me redefine and redesign the Inn, and thus it began to change again. I believe, because of the influence of your story, and our discussions, the greatest changes are coming, blessed changes.

"I'm inclined to thank you for these changes, but that would not be right. I know that the influence, and guidance for change is coming from the Lord. He is guiding us toward some purpose we cannot see right now. We just need to believe."

"My innkeeper, my friend. That is deep and that is an expression of your belief I have not heard before. I agree with all you have said, and I would encourage you to spend time with Mara, I mean Naomi, sharing these kinds of thoughts and ideas, prayerfully, and may the Lord bless you and keep you. Incidentally, you know her real name is Naomi, and she is inclined to embrace it. It's a good change, and I encourage you to reinforce it.

"Now, I must tell you that it's time for me to go. I'll be traveling first to Bethany, where I'm hoping to meet up with Matthias. Then I'm going to take my life in my own hands and go into Jerusalem to meet with followers the Jesus. I want to hear firsthand what they have to say about meeting with Jesus after he was executed on that cross. A resurrection. That is something I am still struggling with, but I have to believe it happened because I believe those who told us, and I believe that Jesus is a man of God."

"Shimon, I agree with you. When I heard what they did to Jesus, my first reaction was shock, and then his dying. Then, just days later, we learned of the resurrection through Matthias. I found that so hard to understand. I'm sure we will learn more as time goes by, what it all means.

"My friend, I'm sorry to see you go, but I understand the need for you to be home. You have a ministry, a blessed ministry. But please know that you are welcome here, anytime."

"Abbas, I intend to travel this way sometime in the future, maybe next year. I'll write to you and Naomi and keep you informed what I'm doing, and I hope you'll do the same. For now, I must prepare to be on my way."

The two stood and embraced, and the irony of that show of friendship was not lost on either one.

Chapter 41

NAOMI'S RETURN

She walked out of the Inn and sat on a bench, repeating her name, Naomi, testing it out, as if it were brand new. Far up the road toward Bethany she could see Shimon leading his horse. She was going to miss him. She wanted to know more about his experience and how it affected him. What more would he learn when he meets with members of The Way? It would be risky for him to go into Jerusalem, but he will do that. She whispered a little prayer, "Stay safe."

As she had been listening to what Shimon had to say, there was something that touched her deeply. It was more than his experience. It was something about that man of God, Jesus, the one that was Crucified and, according to the stories, was resurrected. What was important about the resurrection? Did it confuse her? No, she was not confused about that. In fact, she was certain that belief in the resurrection would resolve any confusion for her. What would happen to her if she talked with witnesses, members of The Way? Would she learn more? Would it change her? She had to think about that.

But what was it that seemed to mean so much? Then it became clear. It wasn't any one thing, it was everything. What Shimon had described, made her feel as if God was working within her. The resurrection was a confirmation of all that she had heard about Jesus, all the stories, the miracles, all of it became real when Jesus walked out of the tomb. The forgiveness of all the brokenness, the healings, all were signs that she, too, was healed and forgiven. She felt clean, she felt new. And the tears came, tears of joy and renewal. She was a new person, and it wasn't just the name change.

With an inner peace, she looked out on the familiar view. The road, all browns and tans, rocks, and gravel, nearly level here, then further north, she knew down there the road sharpened into steep and dangerous grades. She had heard all the stories from numerous travelers during her years of living and working at the Inn. Her gaze took in the valley, the Jordan River, and there, just on the other side, a patch of green and a small herd, maybe of sheep. She felt a calmness, a peace settle within her.

Her mind turned to what Yosef had said about a change in his mind, a change in the direction of his life. What had he said? Yes, that God had intervened and pointed him in a new direction. He had also said something that surprised Naomi; 'I no longer believe as the Sadducees, so I must leave them'. How could he do that? How would he do that? For most of his life he had been a Sadducee, serving in the temple. What would he do?

Naomi knew little or nothing about the work of a Sadducee, or the conflict in thought between the Sadducee and the Pharisee. Could he simply return to being a Pharisee? How does that happen? This new direction that God has given him; how would he handle all of that? This was something that Shimon had said that Yosef had to resolve for himself.

Naomi stood and stretched. She was beginning to have thoughts, thoughts about how her life was changing. How long had it been since that time when she was alone? Ten years. She recalled with long-remembered pain that awful shack she lived in near the Dung Gate. How it was impossible to forget the smell of that place, it was constant, often keeping her awake. She had only a vague recollection of Roman soldiers coming and taking her father away. She could not recall her father's face. She did remember feeling afraid and hiding behind her mother. She thought about the time, years later, when she noticed the affliction that would take her mother's life, just at the start. First, eruptions on her face and arms. Finally, she, too, was taken from her life, and she recalled, like a nightmare, those months of panic, after her mother was gone.

Running away, searching in vain, resisting the help of others, finally, the hunger and begging for food. What an awful time that had been!

She did recall her mother's smile, her soft voice, and the warm safety of her loving embrace. Oh, even today, she missed her mother!

Then she thought of the pack of other homeless children, all alone, yet they ran together, begging, stealing, and worse. Where were they now, ten years later? She was sure there would be more on the street today. Who was reaching out to them, as that rabbi had done, so many years ago? Something needed to be done. How could she help? The compassion and the capacity to love of her mother was deeply embedded in her own heart. She would do something.

Something seemed to rattle around in the back of her mind, something that Shimon had talked about. The "what if" times." What if… the stories were true, is what Shimon had said. And those stories were true. What if…those orphan children could be helped? What if…there were others that knew what those children were going through, an experience that I lived. What if…we could get them some help, maybe not parents but regular food and a safe place to stay and sleep. Could the Inn play a role? It certainly was a big part of saving her. I need to think about this…I know I can help!

Then there were thoughts about things of which she had no knowledge. What is there about a Messiah which changes things, everything. Even though she had been exposed to Judaism, she had never been schooled in such things as the Torah and the idea of "The Messiah" was a mystery to her. Why would that make so much of a difference? Why would that cause a Sadducee to change? For that matter, why would something as simple as a basket of bread and fish being handed to him cause a dishonest merchant to alter his thinking and change his whole life?

Someday, she would go to Jerusalem. The thought caused her to smile. *That was ridiculous! A woman alone in that city? Ha! What would I do in Jerusalem? Where would I go? It was a silly idea, far beyond her reach, and yet, it kept coming back to her. Go to Jerusalem! Find the answers to your questions.*

Of course, Yosef had made one suggestion about contacting the women who gathered at the spring, near Damascus Gate, who would help her find the ones she was looking for. Yosef made it clear that if she ever needed help, he would hope to be there, wherever, and whenever that would be. She was not sure about that, considering what Yosef had shared with her.

Then Shimon had told her about something that Matthias had said about going to Capernaum and finding a woman named Mary who was a follower of Jesus. She was beginning to do good work with widows and orphans in that city. So, when the time came, going to Jerusalem, or even to Capernaum, was not out of the question.

Her uncle was standing by the door as Naomi walked back into the Inn.

"Shimon is on his way, Uncle. I'm going to miss him. How about you?"

"Funny you should ask. Shimon and I had that very conversation. Yes, I will miss him, but I suspect he may return sometime, maybe next spring. Did he say anything to you about coming back?"

"Only that he wanted to know what I was planning to do, and that he might return to the Inn later."

Naomi then spent the rest of the morning cleaning rooms that had been occupied. Her busyness covered a sadness in her heart. She surely would miss that Samaritan.

Chapter 42

YOSEF'S DILEMMA

When Naomi was done with her cleaning, she looked in the room where Yosef was now resting comfortably on a bed.

"How are you doing Yosef? Feeling better?"

"Yes, Mara, I am feeling much better, and I thank you for all you have done."

"Yosef, please call me Naomi, my real name. Shimon suggested that it was time to put the past in the past! And I agree."

"Ah, yes, I agree, Naomi is much better. A beautiful name for a beautiful young lady. I couldn't help but overhear part of your conversation with your uncle about Shimon. It did occur to me that Shimon did all the right things, and more. I am indebted to him and to the Inn. He saved my life, and much more. Hearing of his experience has had a powerful effect on me and my thinking. Those things that changed his life, has caused me to examine what I believe.

"There have been added expenses of my being here, especially in this room. I will see that they are made right. I suspect that Shimon did not leave with expenses that were not covered. You just let me know what expenses you incur having me here and, when I get back to Jerusalem, I'll see that it is all made right."

"Yosef," Naomi said, "I keep the accounts and Shimon paid my uncle enough to cover all expenses. You should not worry about that."

"Mara, I mean, Naomi, alright, but I still intend to send along something for you and Abbas.

"Can I share a bit more of my story with you? I may have told you that my father was a teacher and a Pharisee. For a time, he was a member of the Sanhedrin. I was raised in a strict home, following Mosaic Law. I went directly from the rabbinical school into service in the temple, and eventually became a Sadducee. I had very little exposure to life in the city or how people talk, and how bad feelings are spread. What I heard within the temple, I have always taken as truth. I never challenged it, never questioned it. I never even considered that the stories about Samaritans were not true. I had heard many of those stories and so I developed my own negative attitude towards them. I simply believed.

"So, I know why Abbas felt the way he did. When I consider all the travelers, he has hosted in the years he has had this Inn, with all sorts of tales, complaints, and biases. No wonder he has certain ideas about Samaritans. All my life I have shared that bias.

"Then, along comes Shimon, who saves my life, gives me a different perspective and demonstrated true compassion. His experience has informed my thoughts. Now, I must consider the possibility that the resurrection, the resurrection of Jesus, was real. If that is true, then I must also consider the possibility that this Jesus could be the long-awaited Messiah. All this happening as I was here, recovering, with the help of the Samaritan and you. Such a short time for such a major change.

"You may not understand this new dilemma I have, Naomi, but I have to consider the obvious, that all people, including Samaritans, have value," Yosef said with a smile. "I now have a neighbor and a friend who is from Samaria! Do you understand that? How will my fellow Sadducees react to that? That truth alone would cause them to reject me. They may even call it blasphemy!

"When I tell them that I believe the resurrection as a true sign of the Messiah, and that this Jesus of Nazareth, who caused them so much grief, could be a holy man, they may take me to the Gehenna valley and stone me. So, you see Naomi this is more than a dilemma, this is a critical change that I'll have to face as soon as I am able to travel."

"Yes, Yosef, I understand it is serious. I think I can understand some of what you must face. This is what Shimon cautioned us about. It may have been Shimon's experience that changed his life, but his sharing has given us cause to consider the direction of ours. For our lives, also, have changed, maybe because of his story, and it will not be easy, but I think it is what God wants for us. While I would like to leave the Inn, and follow Shimon, and be part of his meeting with The Way, my place, for now, is here.

"My uncle needs me, for a time. What I have learned and how it has affected me, makes me want to spend time with him. This is important for him, for me and for the Inn. The purpose of this Inn is hospitality. Welcoming people who are traveling on a very difficult and dusty road. Seeing that they have a clean, safe, and comfortable place to rest and refresh. We must be welcoming all people, not just the Jews that are traveling to Jericho and back. Yes, there will be Roman guardsmen on the road, but they have never been a problem, and there will be others.

"My uncle's attitude toward Shimon, when he found out that he was a Samaritan, embarrassed me, at first. But you know he is coming along, and he and Shimon had a surprisingly friendly conversation just before he left. So, I must spend time with my uncle, maybe remind him of some of the things we learned from Shimon."

"Naomi, give him some time. I believe that he did hear much of what Shimon shared with us, and it will take some time to digest. I do think it would be helpful if you could talk with him about how what you have learned has affected you and your thinking. Clearly Abbas loves and respects you. Sharing your thoughts and feelings with him could have a very positive impact on him. Have some patience. Remember, somewhere in the middle of all of this is God. Keep that in mind."

"Of course, Yosef. Now I had better get back to my duties before my beloved uncle snarls at me!" Naomi said with a smile, as she left the room.

Chapter 43

SHIMON IN BETHANY

It was mid-afternoon when Shimon rode to the outskirts of Bethany. From this vantage point, on the slope of the Mount of Olive, he could look down on the city of Jerusalem, the Eastern gate was closest, then west to the far end of the wall and the Damascus gate. He found irony in the fact that he was now preparing to enter this city, a city that, in the past, he dreaded even going around it. Now he would not only enter the city but would find his way through back-streets to a house that Matthias had told him about, where followers of Jesus, The Way, would be meeting.

Earlier that day, he had met some of the disciples, and they had told him of their experience in Capernaum where they had seen Jesus alive for the first time since his crucifixion, and what they said took his breath away. *Could it be that we are dealing with God?*

He should have gone into Jerusalem with John and Peter. It would've been safer. But he had much to tell Matthias, so he stayed. He wanted the disciple to know how Yosef was struggling with all that he was going through. He told him about the injuries and how they had almost healed, and that the rabbi was determined to return to Jerusalem, to his family, as soon as possible, and there were many risks involved.

He also wanted Matthias to know about Naomi, her newfound faith, her background, and her dreams of a mission helping orphans. Shimon thought she had a purpose given by God, to work in Jerusalem or Capernaum, but she wanted to be with followers of Jesus, for guidance and support.

Matthias had said, "I know there are things you want to tell me, but I have some things I must tell you, first. A confession. I am a follower of Jesus and have been for nearly two years. I led you to believe I was one of his twelve disciples, his closest friends. I wish that had been true. Jesus always made me feel like we were dear friends, but I have not been with him throughout his whole ministry. Jesus and the disciples came by my synagogue on their way to Bethesda. I followed him, and I was there on the hillside when he fed the thousands. It was a miracle. I left my position of rabbi then and have been with him ever since. I was not at the Last Supper, that was the Twelve, and John and Peter told us about that later. I was with the disciples in Capernaum when he first revealed that he was the Son of God. I was blessed to be in that meeting room later with disciples and followers when Jesus made himself known to all of us.

"I witnessed Jesus' arrest in the Garden of Gethsemane. After that, so many of us fled the city or hid out. We only heard about the trial, and the awful crucifixion. Only John and Mary stayed there on Calvary in support of the mother of Jesus.

"Shimon, something happened between Jesus' death and burial and his resurrection that I want you to know about. The day after the crucifixion, we were gathered in the safe house. We were all shocked, heartbroken, and fearful. There was great weeping and sadness. We had lost our master; he was dead and buried. This was going on all afternoon. I didn't know what to do. Peter sat in a corner, his head down, crying. Others were concerned about him and told me that he was blaming himself for the death of our Lord.

"But then I noticed Jesus' mother. She was slowly making her way around the room, speaking to each of us, saying encouraging words. When she came to me, she smiled, touched my cheek and, quietly said something about 'God's Son.' I missed part of it. We all thought that she meant that Jesus was now with God. It was later that we realized that Mary was sharing her conviction that Jesus was, indeed, God's Son, and all of this was part of God's plan.

"Shimon, I am sure you have heard the stories about God coming to Mary at the time of her pregnancy. She raised Jesus. All His life there had been signs which she thought was God watching over Him. I am sure it seemed like such a fantasy that most people rejected. But now, what can I say? We believe that Jesus is God's Son, and that changes everything. Think about that, my friend.

"Shimon, I know you want to spend time in Jerusalem with The Way, but, beyond that, what are your plans? You have a very strong experience which you have shared, and I'm sure has had an impact on those people at the Inn. I can only imagine, it has impacted your thinking and planning, when you return to Tirzah. Can you tell me a little bit about that?"

"Oh, Matthias, I can't say that I have a plan. I'm beginning to think that my experience must be shared with others but I'm not sure how to do that. I think there are a lot of people in Samaria who would be eager to hear about this, who would want to know about The Messiah. I guess you could say Samaria is a broad mission field for me. I'll need to give this a great deal of prayerful thought."

"Shimon, when you're meeting with The Way, I hope Philip will be there. You should have talk with him. He will be staying in Jerusalem for a while helping John and Peter organize the growing number of followers. I do know that he has family living in the Caesarea area and I believe he eventually intends to establish a home church there. I don't know when he plans to go, but that's something you can explore with him. Samaria is, as you put it, a broad mission field."

"I appreciate knowing about Philip. It would be most helpful to have a colleague nearby in our work. I'll look forward to talking with him.

"While we are on the topic of plans, what are yours, Matthias? When we first met, you were sharing your experience with the family of Zacchaeus, in Jericho. I got the impression that you thought that was something you could do well, to the benefit of others, which seems to me to be a mission of sorts. Any thoughts about where that might take you?"

"Shimon that's interesting that you should raise that question. Peter asked me to consider returning to Judea and visiting the small villages there, telling them of the work of our Lord Jesus. Maybe gather some of the people and form a church. That has some appeal. But you know, Shimon, I have always favored going east and settling in the Caspian Sea area. I have spent time there. It's a beautiful area, with lots of villages. So, I guess I would favor doing mission work there. I think my family would like it. Time will tell."

Their conversation was interrupted when Martha invited them to lunch. So, Shimon and Matthias, sat down with the sisters and their brother, Lazarus. During that meal, the story of Jesus freeing Lazarus from the tomb was described in detail. Once again Shimon had the strong feeling that they were indeed dealing with the presence of God.

After the meal, Shimon spoke briefly about Yosef and Naomi, and Matthias pledged to look in on them in the next few days. Then he walked Shimon to the edge of the village, where Matthias pointed to the near gate, and said, "That is Golden gate, where Jesus entered at the start of Passover week. It leads directly into the Temple Mount and will be crowded. Instead, follow the wall west and you come to the Damascus gate. That one leads into the marketplace. Turn right and you'll find the street you want."

Shimon mounted his horse and started down the hill. In two miles, he would be at Damascus Gate. It was with a mix of apprehension and excitement at the prospect of being in Jerusalem and meeting with members of The Way.

Chapter 44

I AM THE WAY

Shimon held his horse to a slow trot. He would be in Jerusalem soon enough. He thought how God had directed his steps these past months since he first started hearing stories of Jesus. What an unexpected, even spiritual, experience it has been.

He had to smile at the irony, he, a Samaritan, had saved the life of a Sadducee. No, it was not something that he had done, it was something that God had done through him. The strength and resolve that enabled him to help Yosef, were all the Lord's doing. Yes, he knew, and in knowing, he again, thanked God. Something he seemed to be doing, frequently.

He knew his life began to change before he was aware of it. People were surprised as they watched him and listened as he shared his experience, talking about those stories of Jesus, explaining, in part, why he was a different person. During that time, more and more fellow Samaritans had been drawn to his home wanting to talk to him and hear about his travels. He had been surprised, but gradually realized that in telling of his experiences, he was sharing something special.

He thought again about all that had happened on his travels; the stories, the miracle in Gadara, his conversations with Matthias, what happened in Jericho, on the road and at the Inn. It was more than helping Yosef. He had been inspired to share his experiences with Yosef, Naomi, and Abbas. That had been powerful to put it all together, all that Jesus had done in his life. He did not know how hearing his story would affect them into the future, but he did know it was all in the hands of the Lord.

Jesus had spoken about making disciples. He wasn't sure what that meant, until one man explained that, if we believe, we are to tell others what we believe, sharing Jesus' teachings, and how they were reflected in the way his life had changed. At first it sounded too simple, but now, after this experience, and what had been happening back in Samaria, he knew that there was wisdom in that explanation.

Shimon knew that without the help of the spirit, he could not have accomplished anything. He offered prayers of gratitude for giving him the words that described the power of God's touch in saving his life and changing him, for he believed that sharing that experience is what God intended. He thought again of Abbas, Naomi, and Yosef, knowing that he had no idea what they may do with the knowledge of his experience, but, again, he was confident it was in God's hands".

Once he arrived in Jerusalem, he found the home where followers of The Way met. They were being very cautious; meeting in homes, in remote locations, with the doors and windows locked, fearful of the Romans and the Pharisees. Word of Jesus' resurrection had spread and, while some believed, others didn't, and threats against Jesus' followers had grown.

Some of the disciples had wondered why he, a gentile from Samaria, would follow Jesus, and return, where threats were everywhere. It was only after he told them of his experience in Gadara, the teaching, and the feeding of the crowd, that they began to accept him. He met Philip and Barnabas, and others.

He learned from the witnesses, the truth of the resurrection and absorbed the belief that Jesus was, indeed, The Messiah. They told him of their experience with the risen Jesus earlier that week, and the charge to share the teachings of the master. He learned of the sad death of Stephen, stoned for professing his belief in Jesus. They all had to be careful.

They talked through the night and the more Shimon heard, the more convinced that his mission was to return to Samaria and follow

Jesus' ministry, by sharing the lessons Jesus taught, telling of his own experience, and all he had learned from the disciples.

He had a good conversation with Barnabas who helped him understand more fully the power and meaning of the resurrection. The elder disciple made it clear that he had no doubt that Jesus was The Messiah, promised by God and recorded in the Holy Writ.

"Shimon, you should understand that we are disciples of Jesus, the Messiah. We call ourselves The Way because that is exactly what Jesus told us. Very early on he said *I am the way the truth and the life*, and at the time we weren't sure what that meant. But, over the years of his ministry, we began to realize that there is only one way to God and that is through Jesus. So, Jesus is The Way."

"Barnabas, I had never heard it explained, thank you. The Way, the truth, and the life. Yes, that sounds right. So many of the stories of Jesus ministry that I have heard over the past few years, which I doubted, are now real to me. Matthias verified that the things that I had heard, and even some of the things that I had seen, we're all true. And now you're explaining this to me and it is so right."

During his time in Jerusalem, Shimon had talked with many of the disciples and was overwhelmed by all he had learned. What Barnabas had told him, touched him deeply. Yes, he, too, believed that Jesus was The Messiah.

As Shimon was preparing to leave Jerusalem to return to his home, Barnabas told him he was planning to travel to Antioch, sometime in the future, and that he would stop in Tirzah on his way and would look forward to meeting with a gathering of the Samaritans, Greeks, and gentiles, all who believed. Then he invited Shimon and Philip to come to Antioch and learn of the power of the Gentile Church, an invitation that would be accepted within the year.

It was with a sense of peace and purpose, that Shimon mounted his horse and guided it through the same gate he had entered with some anxiety, just two nights before. Now he was going home, home to Samaria.

Chapter 45

THE SADDUCEE AND THE DISCIPLE

While Shimon was leaving Jerusalem, Yosef was walking into the dining room of the Inn. It was early morning. He was wearing a borrowed tunic and sandals, and he walked with just a slight limp. His healing was nearly complete.

Naomi greeted him and pointed to a table where a man, Yosef had never seen before, was sitting. As he approached the table, the man stood, smiled at him saying, "Are you Yosef? My name is Matthias. We have a mutual friend, Shimon. I saw him a few days ago, and he said you were healing from some injuries and that you were planning to travel to Jerusalem, maybe even today. Are those still your plans?"

Yosef considered this, before answering. "How do you know Shimon?"

"Actually, I've only known Shimon for just a short time. We first met in Jericho, then later in Bethany, when he was getting medical supplies needed for, I would guess, you. I am a disciple of Jesus of Nazareth, the one that was crucified, the one they are now calling The Messiah. I'm from the region of Galilee, but now I am staying in the home of friends, Lazarus, and his sisters, in Bethany.

"Yosef, I'm familiar with Shimon's story, for it is so much like my own. I'll tell you more, but let's sit and have a bit of breakfast, that this young lady has prepared. She and I had a brief chat before you arrived and I know that she, too, has heard Shimon's story and felt its impact."

"Yes, let's eat. You say your name is Matthias?"

"Yes, that is less complicated than my Hebrew name. You see, I'm the son of Tolmai, who was the rabbi for Capernaum for many years. After he passed away, I became the rabbi in the synagogue of a small town just north of Bethsaida, in Galilee. I first heard about the man Jesus from Rabbi Ashraf of Nazareth nearly three years ago. I went to Jesus' house, just outside of Capernaum, a house that he had built with his own hands. I was curious to know what he was teaching and marveled at the crowd that had gathered. I really liked what he had to say, and I kept coming back to listen to Him."

"You were a rabbi? Did you ever make pilgrimage to the Great Temple in Jerusalem?"

"Oh, yes, every year, first with my father, then on my own, until two years ago. That is when I realized that I believed what Jesus was teaching, and I stepped away from my duties as rabbi. That was a real struggle for me and for my family. It was upsetting to some of the people in temple, but by that time many others were followers of Jesus, as well."

"That is very interesting. How did your wife and family react when you told them? I am very concerned about telling my family about this experience and how my beliefs are changing."

"Yosef, how they will react is in the hands of God. My wife was very quiet, then she told me she needed to return to the home of her parents to pray and think about what I had been telling her. She was gone but a few days. When she returned, she asked me to forgive her for leaving me alone with my thoughts. Then she said something very wise and very true. She said that if the spirit was speaking to me, there could be no conflict with the Law of Moses because all of it was God-given. She then vowed that she had no conflict with what my spirit and heart were telling me, for we were one in the eyes of God. She said we would face the synagogue and the world together, and we have. As for my children, they are young, and they are being brought up in a godly home.

"Yosef, of course I do not know anything about your wife or your children, but I have great faith in God. Place your decisions in his hands, for He can carry you through. Trust Him.

"Shimon told you about his encounter with Jesus, and the miracle of feeding the crowd. I was there, Yosef, on that hillside, not far from my home. Then we had this awful time in Jerusalem, during Passover, Jesus' death and then the glory of his resurrection. We don't know where all this will end, we just know that this is all part of God's plan. Whatever happens is in His hands. Which is why I am heading back to Bethany to stay for a while.

"Shimon tells me you are a Sadducee and a member of the Sanhedrin. That you were beaten and robbed on your way to Jericho. He also said that you may be struggling with what he had shared with you. Is that true?"

Yosef, gave that some thought, then nodded in agreement, saying, "Yes and no. I am struggling and praying about this. But I have come to realize that God is in all this – the difficult decisions, the complications, even the consequences. God is in all of it. Last night I prayed that He would help me. You might be part of His answer to my prayers."

"Well, we shall see. I am here because in my heart I believe that my Master wants me here talking to you, and I promised Shimon that I would come to the Inn and check on you. I will be going to Bethany and, later, on to Jerusalem. He also said that you might be going into the city about the same time.

"I got to thinking about what he said about you getting over injuries, and you might be considering some hard decisions. So, I decided to come down and see if you would like company and conversation for the few miles back to Bethany. Then I would meet with my friends in the afternoon. What do you think? I don't want to impose on you, I just thought you could use some company, maybe just to test out how well you could travel."

"Well, Matthias, having company would be good. I think I am strong enough to travel, but it wouldn't hurt to test that. You are right about the hard decisions I am facing, the result of Shimon's story and good deeds, and my own conflicts.

"How can I have changed so radically in what I believe, in this short span of time? It's not the injuries or the robbery that has made the difference. I think that my own dislike, maybe hatred, for Samaritans was shaken. I have held a prejudice against those people all my life, and then suddenly I met one that showed me compassion, and caring. I'm ashamed to say it, but I didn't know how to handle it, at first.

"When I think about my duties in the Temple, and what I am and what I have been. Then consider what I, myself, have experienced, and why I experienced it. How do I answer this talk that Jesus is the Messiah? I am educated in the Talmud and know that resurrection is a sign of The Messiah. But Jesus of Nazareth? Really? A rabbi who is a carpenter? Does that make any sense? That is part of my conflict."

Matthias thought about that as he poured hot tea into cups for them. "Does it make sense? No. Is it God's will? We shall see. What do I think? Yosef, I have watched the master through two years of His ministry. I have seen Him heal the afflicted, I was in a boat on the Sea when he quieted the storm, and I witnessed Lazarus's return to life. When I saw Him on the hillside near Capernaum, after he was dead and buried, forgiving Peter, and telling us to be at peace, any doubt I may have had was gone. In my mind and in my heart, Jesus of Nazareth is the Messiah.

"Yosef, the struggle you are having, the conflict you are working through is God given. Pray and surrender it to Him. I vividly recall my own conflict. I have been a member of The Way for most of the past year. It was a real change from being a rabbi, but I thank the Lord for bringing me in contact with John, Peter, and Matthew. They have helped me greatly in sorting out the confusion of what I believe, and then to understand the new mission that I am now on.

"Now, let's have some of this fine food that Naomi has put before us, to strengthen ourselves for the journey ahead, before we continue our conversation."

Chapter 46

TWO MASTERS?

They were silent while they ate, and then as they sipped their tea, Yosef said, "Let me change the subject a bit and ask what Shimon told you about me?"

"Well, Yosef, he didn't tell me much of anything, except that you had an encounter with some dangerous people and were wounded. Knowing Shimon, he shared with you his own recent experience and his encounter with Jesus. He probably explained how much that encounter had changed his life, and how he continued to have a powerful need to reach out to others. All of that is very true and meaningful.

"He did tell me you were a Sadducee and that you might have some continuing questions. You mentioned you had a conflict, and you have talked about part of it. Is there more you would like to say about that?"

"I have a basic question, Matthias. Can I serve two masters? One that I have been part of all my life, that provides support for my family, but a master I no longer believe in. The other is a growing spiritual influence that has clarity, purpose, and, dare I say, love. That is my conflict."

"Yosef, I was a rabbi for several years, and before that I was raised by a teacher of the law and rabbi, my father. Together we saw many examples of disingenuousness within our congregations. Those who could talk strong faith in God, but outside the synagogue did not reflect that. Often a rabbi gets discouraged because we do see the hidden side of our congregation and where the flaws are, and we do our best to minister to them. When Jesus came into my life, I found I simply had to follow him. It was more than what he said, it was who he is, even before this recent revelation. The change required hard decisions by me and a difficult choice for my wife. Yosef, it boils down to faith and strength of character. The choice is always yours.

"That might not be of great help, except to verify that your conflict is real. Let me share one more thing that was helpful to me in resolving my own conflict. I went back to the Talmud, to Genesis, where it talks about Abraham and Isaac. As you know, Yosef, it is a story of righteousness and faith in God. For me it was like a light was shown on the darkness of my conflict and I found my decision in prayer. I shall pray for you, Yosef, that this conflict is resolved and that you will find your purpose, the one that God has planted within you. Let me think about that, Matthias. But tell me, what is this new mission of yours?"

"Well, the reason that I am going to Bethany is to meet with some people who are trying to understand Jesus' ministry. Many of these people have heard a little of Jesus teachings, maybe just stories, and they want to hear more. Some had witnessed amazing events in recent months.

"I am looking forward to a conversation, and an opportunity to share our stories of Jesus with them. There will be some in the group that feel that they are lost, and they want to believe in something. So, what I do is relate to their conflicts, because I have been there, then I tell them what it has meant to be a believer and a disciple. I believe that is my mission.

"Yosef, think about this. Where you are in your conflict is like where so many are. Why not come with me to Bethany, listen to what they have to say, and what I would tell them. Maybe that would help you think through this change in your life."

"Matthias, I would like to listen to the conversation and the questions they have, because I suspect, that many of their questions are the same ones I have.

"I have been considering all that Shimon had shared. For the past several days I have been going back and forth between what my heart says and what my mind is saying, until last night. Last night, as I stood looking out over the valley and to the sky full of stars, I believe that the spirit of the Lord touched me and, for the first time, I knew that I didn't have a real conflict, I was simply avoiding the obvious. I believe what Shimon had shared, and now I must undertake some difficult decisions.

"I will explain all this to my family, for my decisions will affect them. After that, I will speak to the Sadducee council, and simply tell them that I must remove myself from their numbers. I don't know how they will react, but I am anxious. I have seen the Council very angry, and I heard about Stephen's testimony, and his death. So, you can see I have every reason to be anxious.

"After that, I will see what God would have me do, next. Maybe we can talk about that as we travel, and you can tell me further about your own experience that led you to leave your congregation and become part of The Way. Your wife's reaction seems very supportive. I am not certain how my wife will react. My children, too, are young and they will come to understand.

"Matthias, thank you for coming down and reaching out to me. I think I am physically strong enough to make the journey, but having company, especially here to Bethany, and joining you with that group, for a time, would be very helpful. I would like to know more about Lazarus and how that happened.

"Now, I need to speak to Naomi and Abbas, and let them know how grateful I am to them and that I will be leaving."

Chapter 47

SYCHAR

Meanwhile, some twenty miles west of Jerusalem, Shimon rode on, heading back to Tirzah, his shop, and his home. The gentle swaying was always encouragement for him to ponder things that had happened, or things said, and now he was replaying the discussions yesterday in Jerusalem with the disciples.

They had talked at length about the last supper with Jesus when he explained what was going to happen to him and how it would it affect all of them. But it was what they heard Jesus say when he was breaking the bread, that confused them. He had used the bread and the cup of wine as symbols for his own body that would be broken for them. They didn't understand what he was talking about until three days later, when their lives were shaken with Jesus' crucifixion, his body broken and nailed to the cross. But it was later, in Capernaum, when several of them witnessed the resurrection and saw Jesus alive, that they began to understand. Even now they were struggling to understand their part in God's on-going plan.

Shimon had listened carefully as they debated what Jesus meant when he spoke of making disciples of all nations. It was Peter who offered the notion that what Jesus meant had to do with building community, gathering those of like thought, into homes, forming churches. Strengthening one another. That seemed right.

Barnabas had taken it a step further, and reminded them of Jesus' parable of the seeds, and that making disciples could mean living our lives according to His commandments, and showing others the way to truth, love, and the fullness of life. Those comments caused general agreement by all gathered there.

To Shimon, it all made sense, and caused him to wonder, what community do I have in Tirzah? He remembered neighbors who sought him out, who had come to talk about his experience and the stories that he was sharing. Could that be a community? Is that what Jesus was talking about? Could he start a church in his home? What would his friend Nahman say? That thought caused him to smile.

He then recalled something that had happened just before he left on this market journey. Those people from Sychar or Shechem that had come into his shop to buy silk cloth. They, too, were talking about Jesus coming to their village and the change that had occurred because of his presence. They told him what had happened, and he had shared some of the stories that he had heard earlier. At that time, he wasn't sure they were true, but now, however, that had changed.

He would soon be crossing the border into Samaria, and, in his mind, he knew the route to Tirzah, but, a slight detour could lead him to Jacob's Well. There he could try to locate those people. He remembered one name, Photini, the woman who first talked with Jesus. He paused and thought about taking the detour. It would add to his travel, but that didn't concern him, he had time. There might be value in understanding what had happened to that little village after Jesus, The Messiah, had visited. He shouldn't pass up another opportunity as he had in Afula, so, when he reached the road that led Sychar, without another thought, he turned his horse, and took the detour.

It was midafternoon when Shimon arrived at Jacob's Well. Several women were there, talking and filling water jars. He tried to speak to them, but they turned away, and one of them cautioned the others do not speak to him.

Shimon called after them, "I am looking for a woman named Photini. She, and others from your village came to my shop in Tirzah and made some purchases. They said something special had happened here, and I just wanted to talk further with her."

One woman turned and said, "You're that merchant? Photini told us about stopping in your village, before continuing to the port on the Great Sea. She said she tried to explain to you what happened in our village, but you didn't seem interested. She also told us some of the stories that you had shared, stories that she thought you didn't believe. Stories that we know to be true. Are you that man?"

"Yes, I am, and you are right, Photini and the others were excited about what had happened here, and, at the time, I have to say I was very skeptical of what they were telling me. The stories I was sharing, I thought they were fables. But that was then, and since, I have had reason to believe all those stories are true and that you folks here in this village are correct, Jesus is the Messiah. His resurrection more than a week ago would seem to prove that.

"Do you know where I can find her? Photini? Will she be coming to the well?"

The woman looked to the others, before she continued, "Yes, she's always the last to arrive because of her mission. She will be here. You just stay where you are."

"You said 'her mission'?" Shimon inquired.

"Since Jesus visited our village, Photini has become a leader in our community. She has shared our experience with Jesus to other villages. Here in our town, she reaches out to those families that don't have the capacity to make the journey to the well to get water. Twice a week, she comes with her donkey cart and picks up water jars from those families, comes here, fills them, and then delivers. She always says, 'don't thank me, thank Jesus'. She truly is a saint.

"Ah, there she is. I told you she would be here." She and the other women walked to the well where a woman stopped her cart, loaded with jars, near the well and started to fill them, with help from the other women.

Shimon called out, "Can I help?"

Their answer was "No! You stay where you are."

The women chatted as they worked, and one of them gestured toward Shimon, standing by his horse.

He recognized the woman as the one who had been at his shop. The task completed, Photini lead her donkey to a patch of grass and tethered it, then turned her attention to Shimon. "What brings you here to our humble village. We have no real marketplace for a merchant like you," she said.

"Photini, greetings. I am Shimon, and, yes, we met some time ago at my shop in Tirzah. You bought silk cloth and some perfume, as I recall. You and your friends we're excited to talk about what happened in your village because of the visit by Jesus, The Messiah. I must confess that at the time I was skeptical of what you told me, but then, I didn't believe the stories that I was sharing with you. I now regret that doubt and would like to hear again about your village."

Photini and the other women approached together and proceeded to talk in detail about what had happened during those days of Jesus' visit and then the weeks and months since. It was a gratifying story, one of discovering love and respect for one another, of restoring broken relationships, and forming new ones.

Photini said, "We smile! We never smiled before. We were always guarded and distant. It felt so good to relax and feel the warmth of friendship. Oh, there were some who were still grumping, but we don't let them bother us. In the past, I was always cut off from these women, they never knew about my life. But now we share, and we hug! Oh, and there is trust. We trust one another. That is so good.

Another woman, pointed to Photini, and said, "Our sister, here, our friend, has been through so much in her life, sadness, and grief. But she is strong, and has so much compassion, we look up to her and she encourages us to reach out to others. She calls that her mission and tells us that our Messiah had blessed her. Our Messiah! Imagine that!"

And so, the conversation continued until all the women had added to the story of Jesus transforming their village, and all who live there. Shimon began to realize that a simple visit by Jesus to the Well had truly made a difference for all those living here, a blessing. A blessing that caused Shimon to call to mind those conversations there at the Inn, all inspired from his encounter with Jesus, on a hillside, near the

"I believe that all the followers of Jesus, were shocked and grieved at his execution, and then, most recently, you celebrated His resurrection. Please know, I share that, I am just learning, trying to understand what it means for me and my family.

"I have so many questions, because I know that in the next few days, I will be faced with whatever consequences may come when I step away from my role in the Temple and speak with my wife and children. I know that the Sanhedrin will not take kindly to me, when I remove myself from their numbers. So, I'm here to learn, and I'm hoping that our discussion will help me resolve this struggle I am having. You have nothing to fear from me, not now and not in the future. Please allow me to stay and listen, and maybe to raise my own concerns."

There were nods of acceptance from the group, then the conversation continued for nearly two hours. Yosef listen intently as more and more of the questions he had in mind were discussed, some resolved and some continued. He was amazed when a woman, Martha, spoke of the grief she felt at the death of her brother and her frustration when Jesus did not come to heal him. She described the shock the mourners felt when he came and ordered the tomb opened, and her brother, after four days, walked out, alive! What an inexpressible joy she experienced. It was a miracle, an act of God. Her brother, Lazarus, sitting right there, next to her, could only nod.

Yosef took all this into his heart and was beginning to realize how powerful an experience he had, every part of it from being attacked, to being saved, both physically and spiritually. The witness offered by Shimon, his own belief struggle, and now, to hear the witness of the sister whose brother was brought back from the grave. What was he to think?

As the gathering closed with prayers, Matthias tapped him on the shoulder and said, "Yosef, you didn't raise any questions. Has this been helpful? Or, has what you have heard simply complicated your struggle?"

"Oh, Matthias, this has been so important to me. I didn't need to raise my questions because they were raised by others. And Martha's testimony about her brother, caused tears to flood my eyes. I am so glad to have met you, to have you come by the Inn and now introduced me to these wonderful people, fellow followers of Jesus the Christ. Did I say, 'fellow followers?' Thank you."

"This is all the work of our Lord, and we should thank Him every day," Matthias said. "Will you be alright to continue on to Jerusalem and your home?"

"Oh, yes, I'll be fine. God bless you, Matthias. I'm confident that our paths will cross again. Now I must be on my way home, I have much to share with my wife, Deborah, and it will be good to see my children." Then he turned, left the house, and started down the hill toward the Damascus Gate and Jerusalem.

Chapter 49

DREIDELS AND RAISONS

It was late afternoon when Yosef arrived in Jerusalem. He chose to go directly home, instead of going to the temple, because he wanted to see his wife and children. It was hard for him to realize that it had been nearly three weeks since he left home. So much had happened to him and now his thinking was changed and, that, in turn, will cause all their lives to change.

The reunion was joyful and active, despite his continuing aches and pains. He told his wife, Deborah, and his two young daughters just a bit about what happened to him. How he had been rescued by a good man who happened along, and how he had met some very interesting people at a country inn on the road.

When dinner over, they cleared the table and brought out the dreidels and raisons, for keeping score, all of which brought squeals of delight from the little girls. For the next hour, they spun the tops, ate raisons, and laughed and talked, until the littlest one nearly fell asleep at the table…story time. Once they were tucked in bed, and, before the story ended, both were sound asleep.

He could no longer avoid this most difficult conversation. He prayed silently to the Lord that his wife would understand that she, somehow, would begin to see the truth and the new life that has been laid out for them by God.

Yosef and Deborah sat side by side in the gathering room. She started by saying, "You handled that well with the children. There is only so much they need to know. I'm so grateful that you are here, now, home with us. I can tell your injuries are still healing and I could not miss the times when you moved, awkwardly, with your pain. I have loved you too long for me not to know that there is much that you are not telling. I also know that when you are ready, you will confide in me."

They sat in silence long moments before Yosef, took her hand, and said, "I do have much to share with you, my lovely Deborah. Much of this will be hard for me to say and because of that, I must tell you that I have loved you too long for me not to confide completely, even painfully. I also must tell you that I don't fully understand all that has happened and how my thinking is in the process of changing." And so, he began…

It was quite late when Yosef had shared all that had happened from his being attacked on the road, his life-saving rescue by a very good Samaritan merchant. He shared the conflict of having his life saved by one whose life, in turn, had been saved by Jesus, and whose story touched him, so, as well as the lives of a young woman, and an innkeeper. He spoke of his growing belief in Jesus, and his belief that this new revelation of the resurrection, that was causing so much unrest throughout the city, was true, and a sign that Jesus was The Messiah.

He spoke of not knowing what to do with his position on the Sanhedrin in light of this new conflict, and went on to explain that for him to resume his duties as a Sadducee, while keeping the power of this experience to himself, was impossible. Therefore, he told her, he must resign the council, and deny his birthright as a Sadducee.

They sat, still holding hands, and thought about all that Yosef had revealed. Once again, it was Deborah that broke the silence with a declaration, "Again, I say, I have loved you too long not to know that this experience that you have had will not divide us! Yes, it will bring on changes in our lives, some of which will probably be most uncomfortable, but you and I must remain strong. Our most important concern must be those little ones of ours."

Chapter 50

VISITORS

Over the next few days, it was clear that Deborah had been shocked and equally conflicted by her husband's experience. Yet, she strongly supported him in whatever decision he would make. Later, he sought out his old mentor, Gamaliel, and explained the source of his dilemma, including his long-standing dissatisfaction with Jewish orthodoxy.

While understanding his former student's conflicts, it was clear from his guidance that the hypocrisy of his continuing under the temple culture, would be neither wise nor advised. In his heart, Yosef knew that his place was no longer in the temple, but among those who followed Jesus, the Messiah.

So, it was, a week after his return, he stood before the Sanhedrin and explained his reason for resigning. His statement was met with anger and threats, and he departed the temple. Late that evening, two men arrived at Yosef's front door. It was with a certain degree of trepidation, that he was surprised to see two Pharisees; Joseph, who represented Arimathea, and Nicodemus, one of the elders.

Before he could say anything, Joseph asked for time to speak, assuring him that they did not come to challenge his decision. Yosef invited them in and showed them to the gathering room where Deborah sat. The two nodded respectfully in her direction and simply said "Good evening", then sat down.

Joseph continued, "My colleague and I are here to ask you something, born of our own struggles. We, among others, opposed the violent actions that some advocated against the rabbi from Nazareth, and it grieved us. You may have heard that we claimed the body of the rabbi, Jesus, and saw that he had a proper burial. He was, after all, a Jewish rabbi.

"As you know, we Pharisees believe in the Resurrection, as proclaimed in the Holy Writ. It is a sign of the Messiah. There is much talk in the city that this Jesus is The Messiah. That he rose from the grave and had been seen, multiple times. But we have proof of this. Yes, the tomb is empty. But we have not seen him, nor do we believe he is a true resurrection. Still, my colleague and I remain conflicted."

Nicodemus had been silent, but now spoke, "Yosef, you were part of the Sanhedrin, a year ago, when I spoke to them about my conversation with Jesus. At that time, we called him a mad rabbi. I told the council that I thought what his teaching was too simple. Over this past year, Joseph and I have talked about the many stories we have heard of Jesus' ministry; stories of acts of healing and miraculous things that he has supposedly done. Our colleague on the Council rejects all those stories. My friend and I are not so sure. Our discussions all seem to end with the question we can't answer, 'What if all these stories are true?' Can you help us resolve this uncertainty?"

"Nicodemus and Joseph, you two are among a small number of the Sanhedrin that I look up to for counsel, wise elders that I trusted, even in the face of my own doubts. Can I help you resolve what you call an uncertainty? No, I can't. Deborah asked the same thing, and my answer was the same.

"The four of us have been grounded in the orthodoxy of the Holy Writ, and we followed it all our lives, to this point. For me, I encountered a violent attack and a surprising turn of circumstance that opened my eyes or, I should say, opened my heart and my mind to what I truly believed. The 'uncertainty' that you speak about may be leading you to a different understanding of what you currently believe. You can resist that, you can deny it, but if it is God at work in you, you will never get rid of it, until you embrace it."

For the first time, Deborah spoke, "Yosef has shared an important conversation he had with some who had similar questions and conflicts. which leads me to suggest, if you have an opportunity to spend time with members of The Way, ask them the same question. As for my husband and I, we are glad to hear that you are experiencing this 'uncertainty'. Not because of your discomfort, but because it may lead you to a new and different foundation of what you believe. May our God guide your thoughts."

Chapter 51

GOING HOME

Shimon was again in the saddle, heading home, his mind full of so many events and conversations, things that had happened, things that he had witnessed, had heard. He replayed what the two stablemen had told him, one in Afula and one in Jericho. The healing of the ten lepers and the one that returned, that danced in celebration in the square. The restoring sight to blind Bartimaeus, who followed Jesus to Jerusalem. He realized that he had no doubt that these were acts of the Messiah.

He replayed the conversation he heard there in the dining room in Scythopolis. The words of the man from Pella who said he had participated in the feeding of five thousand and spoke about the powerful experience he had following that miracle that had changed him. Now, Shimon had a similar experience there in Gadara, and knew that was the touch of the Messiah.

He laughed at himself when he recalled saying that "unless I see it, I won't believe it," and then there before his very eyes was the Messiah teaching and feeding another crowd on another hillside, and I was one of those fed! I believe, I believe!

He recalled, with a warmth in his heart, the conversation with Matthias, his dear friend, when the disciple had set him straight, confirmed to him the acts of miracles. It had taken him some time to set aside all his doubts. It was then he realized that the last wisp of doubt had disappeared when he shared his experiences with Yosef, Naomi and Abbas, there in the small storage room of the Inn.

Then those amazing thoughts on the road approaching the Inn, with Yosef on his horse, and the realization that God was in all that he had heard and experienced on his travels. He vividly recalled the sudden epiphany when it had all come together, and in the remembrance, he felt a fresh sense of renewal.

Yes, the Inn on Jericho Road. What an experience! Starting with the confrontation with Abbas, the innkeeper, the blessings of the compassionate Mara, no, not Mara, Naomi. They probably will never forget the man he, a Samaritan, had saved was a member of the Jewish hierarchy. Just an amazing set of circumstances, orchestrated by God.

Then a new thought brought tears to his eyes. The lesson of "doing likewise", a lesson from Jesus, became a real and permanent part of his life, there on that dangerous road when he labored to treat and care for Yosef and then, at the Inn. The effort he made, and the struggles only added to the blessing. Yes, he knew he was blessed, blessed by the Messiah, Jesus of Nazareth. He would return to the Inn one day, but for now, his God-given mission was in Samaria, and so he rode on.

Chapter 52

GOD'S PLAN

The years following Christ's resurrection were chaotic and marked with violence. It was a time of significance, as more and more people were drawn to the spiritual power of His ministry. Forty days following the resurrection, disciples witnessed Christ's ascension. Ten days later, Pentecost, and the gift of the Holy Spirit, the "helper" and "companion" as promised by Jesus, came to those who believe in Christ, injecting power and spiritual growth among believers.

The five years after Shimon and Yosef had traveled from the Inn, were eventful in the growth of Christianity. Just days before Pentecost, Matthias had been elected by the apostles to replace Judas Iscariot as one of the Twelve. True to his commitment to Peter, Matthias visited and encouraged the gatherings of new believers in Judea, before moving his wife and daughters to the Caspian Sea area, where he founded many churches.

Barnabas, now minister to the believers in Antioch began using the term 'Christian' in reference to the mix of cultures and languages of his congregation. From this evolved the term Christianity. Both terms were adopted by the Jerusalem Council in 50 AD.

Home churches were springing up throughout Samaria, through the leadership of Philip and Shimon, beginning with Caesarea and Tirzah. The two spent six months in Antioch with Barnabas learning the role of ministry among diverse congregations.

The foundation of The Way was shaken when Stephen, a deacon in the ministry, was stoned to death, while a firebrand Pharisee named

THE INN ON JERICHO ROAD

Saul watched and encouraged the murder. It would be less than a year later when Saul would encounter Jesus outside Damascus, and he would emerge as one of the most visible leaders in the history of Christianity. Paul went on to declare Christianity as a universal religion, which angered the Jewish hierarchy.

Yosef, more than five years since being attacked on Jericho Road, followed by his resignations from the Sanhedrin and from his birthright as a Sadducee, endured years of threats and struggles, made the hard decision to leave Jerusalem. He and his family, with all their belongings, joined a small Christian community that made its way from Jerusalem, down the road to Jericho, across the Jordan River, into Gentile country, then north to Syria. There they made their home and joined the fledgling Christian community in Pella.

Over the years, his daughters married, had children of their own, and settled nearby, farming and raising herds of sheep. The girls found satisfaction in teaching in the new and growing Christian school. His wife continued to struggle between her Mosaic Jewish roots and belief in Jesus, but nevertheless remained loyal to her husband and did her part to strengthen the community. Yosef found contentment in being an elder and an active teacher in the Christian church.

The impact of Shimon's experience on the hillside near Gadara, and his encounter with Jesus of Nazareth, was like a stone thrown into a placid pool. What started with a carpenter and a simple merchant, gathered power, and that ministry reached out like ripples, touching one life after another, changing each for the better, following Jesus' command to *"go and make disciples of all nations"*.

Photini was greatly impacted by her encounter with Jesus. Her mission was to share the ministry of Jesus, and, over time, she became known as the Mother of Evangelists, her two sisters and two sons became evangelists, and after her death, she was sainted by the Antiochian Orthodox Church (St. Photini).

Over the years, Pella became the destination of Christians leaving Jerusalem and Roman domination in advance of the destruction of the city in 70 AD. By 100 AD Pella had become the center of Christianity, with an estimated population of 7,500. By 200 AD, with a little over three million Christians, the center was moved to Antioch, Syria.

Today, there are 2.18 billion Christians around the world, or a third of the estimated global population! The influence of that blessed carpenter from Nazareth continues to this day.

THE END

APPENDIX A

Chronology of Jesus, the Messiah

The following is an incomplete and generalized chronology of the life and ministry of Jesus of Nazareth, offered in the order suggested from the Bible: Prophecies, scripture details of Jesus' ministry, historic records, and commentaries. This was compiled to advance an orderly understanding of the story of our Lord's earthy life. Each notation is grounded in Biblically supported fact. **Note:** Numbered (#) sites are keyed to Map of the Holy Land found on the next two pages. -- Stan Escott

Jesus, God Incarnate

Circa 1915-1410 BC – Several prophecies foretell of the coming of Jesus, the Messiah:

Genesis 3:15> References an *"enmity between the man and woman because of sin."*

Genesis 12:3> Provides a more specific prophesy of the coming of Jesus, the Messiah. "God told Abram, the father of the Jewish nation, *"All peoples on earth will be blessed through you."*

Exodus 12:12-13> References a bronze serpent on a pole that provides healing.

Circa 700 BC – **Isaiah 7:14>** Isaiah prophecy that the Messiah would be born to a virgin. *"Therefore, the Lord Himself will give you a sign: The virgin will conceive and give birth to a son and will call Him Immanuel."* **Isaiah 53:5-6,** *"He was wounded and bruised for our sins…we have strayed away."*

Circa 600 BC – **Jeremiah 23:5-6**> *"The days are coming, declares the Lord, when I will raise up for David a righteous Branch, a King who will reign wisely and do what is just and right in the land. This is the name by which He will be called: The Lord, Our Righteous Savior."*

Circa 580 BC – **Psalms 22:1**> *"My God, my God, why have you forsaken me?"* Spoken by David, 1,000 years before Christ uttered these words from the cross.

Circa 500 BC – **Micah 5:2**> Micah prophesied that the Messiah would be born in Bethlehem **(2)**, *"But you, Bethlehem Ephrathah, though you are small among the clans of Judah, out of you will come for me one who will be ruler over Israel, whose origins are from old, from ancient times."*

6 BC – **Matthew 1:18-25**> Jesus is born in Bethlehem **(2)**. In Jerusalem **(3)** Jesus is circumcised and dedicated. Joseph, Mary, and Jesus' return to Nazareth **(1)**.

5 BC – **Matthew 2:14-15**> Joseph, Mary and Jesus flee to Egypt **(4)** to escape Herod's orders to kill male infants.

3 BC – **Hosea 11:1** > Joseph, Mary, and Jesus return to Nazareth **(1)** from Egypt **(4)**. Fulfilling Hosea's prophecy that the Messiah would come out of Egypt.

Spring 6 AD – **Luke 2:42-47**> Jesus, age 12, goes with Mary and Joseph to Jerusalem **(3)** for Passover. There he impresses the teachers of the law. **Luke 2:49-52**> *"I must be about my Father's business"*. *"He returned with them to Nazareth **(1)** and was subject until them: but His mother kept all these sayings in her heart."*

6 AD to 27 AD – **Luke 2:39-40**> Little is known of Jesus' childhood and adolescence in Nazareth **(1)**. We assume he was taught in the home

by both Mary and Joseph, but also by rabbis that traveled through the region. It is also assumed that he learned the carpentry trade from Joseph.

Fall 27 AD – **Luke 3:21-22>** Jesus comes to the Jordan River where John is preaching and is baptized by John **(5)**. **The baptism signifies the beginning of Jesus' ministry.**

Winter 27 AD – **John 2:1-11>** Jesus makes first contact with some of John's disciple and draws them into His circle, including Peter, Andrew, Philip, and Nathanael. Later, he attends a wedding in Cana **(6)**, and it is here, at the urging of His mother, Mary, that **Jesus first displays His divine power** by changing water into wine. Mary tells the stewards, and us, *"Whatsoever he saith unto you, do it"* **John 2:5**.

Early Spring 28 AD – **Matthew 4:13>** Jesus moves to Capernaum **(7)**, and His home becomes a gathering place of the early followers.

Spring 28 AD – **John 3:3-9>** Jesus goes to Jerusalem **(3)** for Passover, where his teaching enflames the teachers of the law and Pharisees. Nicodemus meets with Jesus late at night, calling Him "a teacher come from God," yet calls his ministry too unorthodox and mysterious.

Returning to Capernaum, **John 4:25-26, 39-43>** He travels through Samaria **(8)** and has an extensive conversation with Photini, the woman at Jacob's Well **(9)**. Tells her, **"I am The Messiah.** He remains in Sychar **(10)** for two days, gaining followers among the Samaritans.

Late Spring 28 AD – **Matthew 4:18-22>** Jesus returns to Capernaum **(7),** summons the disciples that will be with Him throughout his ministry, including Peter, Andrew, James, and John. His healing and teaching ministry attract many followers.

Summer 28 AD – **Luke 5:17-26>** Jesus travels throughout Galilee **(12),**. His activities become more and more controversial. In the village of

Afula, he heals lepers **(11)**, the untouchables. Jesus is teaching in a house packed with people when men bring a paralyzed friend and lower him through the roof **(7)**. The man is healed. He heals a man on the Sabbath in the Synagogue which causes the Pharisees to consider Jesus dangerous and has to be stopped.

Late Summer 28 AD – **Matthew 5, 6 & 7>** There on the hillside near Capernaum **(13)**, Jesus teaches his disciples in an extensive lesson referred to as the **Sermon on the Mount**.

Fall 28 AD – **Luke 7:12-17>** While traveling near Naim **(14)**, Jesus stops a funeral procession and raises a widow's son from the dead, and the people cry out, *"A great prophet has arisen among us!"*

Matthew 13:9-17, Jesus' teaching is more frequently done with parables. These word-pictures from everyday life appealed to even the most ordinary hearer but carried a deeper insight for "those who have ears to hear."

Winter 28 AD – **Mark 6:14-29>** John the Baptist is executed by Herod **(3)**. This news saddens Jesus.

Mark 4:35-41> Jesus and his disciples are caught in a storm on the Sea of Galilee **(15)**, Jesus speaks, and the storm stops. **Mark 5:21-43>** On arrival in the Gentile Region **(16)**, east of the sea, Jesus heals a man possessed of a legion of demons. Back in Jewish territory, Jesus raises the dead daughter of Jairus the head of a synagogue in Capernaum **(7)**.

Early Spring 29 AD – **Luke 9:1-6, 10-11>** Jesus sends 12 disciples into the villages of Galilee **(12)**, taking nothing but the message of the kingdom of God as taught by Jesus. Weeks later, when they return, the crowds around Jesus grow, even when he seeks privacy.

Spring 29 AD – **Luke 9:12-17>** On a hillside, north of Bethsaida **(17)**, more than 5000 people are fed from a boy's lunch that Jesus has blessed.

These are mostly Jews traveling to Jerusalem **(3)** for Passover. Jesus sends his disciples across the Sea of Galilee **(15)** while he dismisses the crowd. That night they see Jesus walking on the water toward them.

Summer 29 AD – **Matthew 16:13-20>** Crowds follow Jesus into the Gentile and Greek region of Phoenicia **(18)**. Even here his reputation has followed Him. A week later, in the pagan region of Caesarea Philippi **(19)**, Jesus asks what people are saying about Him…" *Who do you believe I am?*" Peter exclaims, "*You are the Christ.*" Jesus and His disciples travel in a wide circle into the cities of the Decapolis **(21)** and then west back to Galilee **(12)**.

Summer 29 AD –**Luke 9:28-36>** That same week, He takes Peter, James, and John to a high mountain (Mount Tabor or Mount Hermon) **(20)**, there they see the transfigured vision of Jesus with Moses and Elijah.

Matthew 6:22-24> Jesus experiences more and more challenges from Pharisees, realizes that opposition to this ministry is beginning to harden, becoming more and more dangerous and he has doubts whether his disciples understand his mission. Jesus begins to tell the disciples he will be rejected, killed, but will rise again. Peter rebukes Jesus for saying such things.

Early Fall 29 AD – **Luke 10:1-20>** Jesus decides to leave Galilee **(12)**, permanently and go to Judea **(29)**, and on to Jerusalem **(3)**. He sends 70 disciples in pairs on ahead of him, preaching the Kingdom of God. When they return, they are fill with joy at what they accomplished. Jesus sees their work as a sign of victory over evil.

Fall 29 AD – **Mark 12:28-34>** Jesus arrives in Jerusalem **(3)** for the Feast of Tabernacles, and his teaching in the Temple arouses more questions and provokes debates whether he is the Messiah.

Luke 10:25-37> He heals a beggar blind from birth, and Pharisees accuse Jesus of deceiving the people on the matter of the Messiah. It is at this time that a lawyer asks about the most important command of the law. Jesus replies to love God with all one's heart, soul, and mind, and the second is to love one's neighbor as oneself. Who is my neighbor? question leads to the parable of the Good Samaritan.

Luke 11:37-44> Still in Jerusalem **(3)**, Jesus is invited to dinner at the house of a Pharisee, but is criticized for omitting the customary handwashing ritual, which leads Jesus to speak on the matter of false piety. He speaks to his disciples on the matter of the ambition of seeking wealth.

<u>Late Fall 29 AD</u> – **Matthew 19:13-14 >**Jesus travels from Judea and across the Jordan River, followed by crowds **(16)**. People begin to bring their children to Jesus for blessings, discouraged by disciples, to which Jesus tells them, "To such belongs the Kingdom of God."

Mark 10:17-22>A rich ruler approaches Jesus with the question, "What must I do to inherit eternal life," and is told to "sell what you have, give to the poor and you will have treasure in heaven. The man leaves saddened.

<u>Winter 30 AD</u> – **Matthew 15:29-39>** Still east of the Jordan **(16)**, but now begins traveling toward Jerusalem **(3)** for Passover. At the village of Gadara **(22)**, he teaches on a hillside where a crowd of more than 4000 has gathered, mostly Gentiles and some Jewish families. Again, he blesses a small amount of food and feeds the crowd. In Jericho **(23)**, he encounters the tax collector Zacchaeus and stays the night with the family and changes the tax collector's heart. He restores sight to blind Bartimaeus as he is leaving Jericho.

<u>Spring 30 AD</u> – **John 11:39-44>** He arrives in Bethany **(24)**, in time for the funeral of Lazarus. He restores life to his friend and spends time with Mary and Martha.

Holy Week –

- Sunday, **Matthew 21:9-11**> Jesus enters Jerusalem **(3)** through the Golden (Eastern gate) gate riding on the colt of a donkey with a large celebrating crowd following. Returns to Bethany **(24)**.

- Monday, **Matthew 21:15**> Jesus is in the Temple, overturning the money changers tables and shouting that this is a house of prayer. Returns to Bethany **(24)**.

- Tuesday, **Mark 14:1-2**> In the Temple, Pharisees and others try to trap Jesus. In the afternoon, Jesus teaches the disciples gathered on the Mount of Olives **(25)**. Referred to as the **Olivet Discourse,** in which he again lays out what would be happening soon.

- Wednesday, **Luke 22:21-23**> Jesus remains in Bethany **(24)**, attends dinner at the home of Simon the Leper (healed), it is here that a woman comes and anoints Jesus from a flask of fragrant nard.

- Maundy Thursday, **Matthew 26:26-30**> In Jerusalem **(3)**, at sundown, Jesus gathers his disciples for the Last Supper, during which he reveals that one would betray him. He uses the bread and wine as a sacrament of remembrance. He then gives them a "new commandment" to love one another as he loves them.

- Holy Friday, **John 18:28-40**> From the Last Supper **(3)**, they immediately gather in the Garden of Gethsemane **(26)** for an early morning time of prayer. Just after midnight, a crowd led by Judas, approach Jesus, and seize him. He is taken to the house of Caiaphas, the high priest. He is taken to Pilate, then to Herod, and then back to Pilate, who offers to pardon Jesus or Barabbas to the crowd, who call for the crucifixion of Jesus. Beaten and scrouged, he is taken to Golgotha **(27)**, nailed to the cross. At 3 p.m. Jesus cries out "It is finished, and Father, I commit my spirit." He dies, and His body is taken by Joseph or Arimathea and Nicodemus and buried in the tomb.

- Holy Saturday, **Luke 23:50-56>** Followers to Jesus spend the day grief-stricken, not knowing what to do.

- Easter (Resurrection) Sunday, **Matthew 28:1-10>** Mary Magdalene and other women go to Golgotha **(27)**, find the tomb empty, and receive a message from an angel that Jesus has risen and would meet disciples near Capernaum **(7)**. Two followers traveling to Emmaus **(28)** encounter the risen Savior, though they do not recognize him.

Four days after the Resurrection, **John 21:4-23>** Jesus meets with five disciples near Capernaum **(7)**, forgives Peter's denials, and dines with them. A week after the Resurrection, Jesus meets with disciples and followers in the upper room in Jerusalem **(3)**. After that meeting, He appears to 500 others in locations unknown.

Forty days after His Resurrection, **Luke 24:50-53>** Jesus took Peter, James, and John from Bethany on to the Mount of Olives **(25)**, where he instructed them to wait in Jerusalem until the arrival of the Holy Spirit when they would His witnesses to the ends of the earth. After He said this, He ascended into a cloud and out of their sight.

Fifty days after His Resurrection, **Acts 2:14-41>** In Jerusalem **(3), t**he person of the Holy Spirit descended upon the apostles, Mary and the followers of Jesus who were all gathered in the Upper Room. The Holy

Spirit now resides in each of us who believe in Jesus, Son of God, a Person of the Triune God.

From that Time and Beyond -- Jesus taught the fundamental moral values of brotherhood and benevolence, which became the central thesis of Christianity. The life and teachings of Jesus Christ are the foundation 'stones' for living a life of a follower of Jesus, Son of God.

APPENDIX B
Map of the Holy Land.

•SIDON

⛰ 20 MOUNT HERMAN
Transfiguration

•TYRE
Heals woman's daughter

•PHOENICIA 18

Galilee 12

•CAESAREA PHILIPPI 19
Visits with disciples
Peter declares him the Christ

Mediterranean Sea

13 SERMON ON THE MOUNT

•CAPERNAUM
• *Many miracles* 7

CANA • 6
Turns water to wine

•BETHSAIDA
Heals a blind man 17
Feeding of the 5,000

•MAGDALA

14 •NAIM

•TIBERIAS
SCYTHOPOLIS•

Sea of Galilee 15

NAZARETH•
Jesus' hometown 1

Cities of the Decapolis 21
Peter, Andrew, John, James fish miracle
Calms the storm
Walks on water
Cast out legion of demons into pigs
Healing miracles
Appears to 7 disciples after resurrection

•AFULA 11

Samaria 8

PORT OF CAESARES
•
• •TIRZAH 31
Home of Merchant

9, 10 *Meets the woman at the well* •SYCHAR

16 Gentile Region

•GADARA 22
Feeding of the 4,000

Jordan River

•EPHRAIM
Seeks refuge after plot to kill him

5 *Jesus Baptized*

ANCIENT ISRAEL
Jesus' footsteps

10 MILES

Judea 29

JERICHO 23
Miracles, including Bartimaeus

28 EMMAUS• 30 •THE INN
⛰ 25
MOUNT OF OLIVES
Taught, prayed, betrayed

JERUSALEM
Palm Sunday
Last Supper •26
Crucified BETHANY
Resurrection 3, 27 *Raises Lazarus* 24
Ascends to Heaven

BETHLEHEM•
Birth of Jesus 2
Massacre of the Innocents

The Dead Sea

----- MERCHANT ROUTE

EGYPT 4

APPENDIX C
Map of the Holy Land. (part 2)

Number	Location and Event
1	NAZARETH - CHILDHOOD HOME OF JESUS
2	- BETHLEHEM - BIRTHPLACE OF JESUS - Massacre of the Innocents
3	- JERUSALEM - SITE OF JESUS' DEDICATION AS A CHILD AND CRUCIFIXION AND RESURRECTION AS AN ADULT - Palm Sunday - Last Supper
4	EGYPT - JOSEPH, MARY AND JESUS FLEE FOR SAFETY
5	JESUS BAPTISM BY JOHN ON RIVER JORDAN
6	CANA - SITE OF JESUS' FIRST KNOWN MIRACLE *Turns water into wine*
7	CAPERNAUM - CENTER OF JESUS' MINISTRY *Many Miracles*
8	REGION OF SAMARIA
9	JESUS MEETS WOMAN AT JACOB'S WELL
10	SYCHAR - JESUS SPENDS 2 DAYS IN TOWN MINISTERING
11	AFULA - JESUS HEALS 10 LEPERS
12	REGION OF GALILEE
13	HILLSIDE NEAR CAPERNAUM - SERMON ON THE MOUNT
14	NAIM - RAISES DEAD SON. "A GREAT PROPHET HAS COME"
15	SEA OF GALILEE
16	REGION OF THE GENTILES
17	- BETHSAIDA – JESUS MINISTRY & FEEDING OF 5,000 JEWS - Heals a blind man
18	REGIONS OF GENTILE PHOENICA
19	- REGION OF PAGAN CAESAREA PHILIPPI - Visits with disciples - Peter declares him the Christ
20	MOUNT HERMON Transfiguration

21	- CITIES OF THE DECAPOLIS - Peter, Andrew, John, James fish miracle Calms the storm - Walks on water - Cast out legion of demons into pigs Healing miracles - Appears to 7 disciples after resurrection
22	GADARA - JESUS MINISTRY & FEEDING OF 4,000 MOSTLY GENTILES
23	- CITY OF JERICHO - JESUS MINISTRY & RESTORE SIGHT TO BLIND BARTIMAEUS
24	- BETHANY - RAISED LAZARUS, HOME OF MARY & MARTHA - Ascends to Heaven
25	MOUNT OF OLIVES - SITE OF OLIVET DISCOURSE BY JESUS
26	GARDEN OF GETHESEMANE - JESUS PRAYS & IS BETRAYED
27	GOLGOTHA - JESUS' CRUCIFIXION & BURIAL
28	EMMAUS - JESUS FIRST APPEARANCE TO TWO MEN
29	REGION OF JUDEA
30	THE INN ON JERICHO ROAD
31	TIRZAH: Home of Merchant SHIMON

ACKNOWLEDGEMENTS

It is difficult for me to find the words to properly acknowledge the role the Holy Spirit continues to play in my writings and all that I do. I can relate to Pastor Robert Lamont, who felt incredibly blessed by God, comparing himself to a turtle on a fence post, that whatever he accomplished in this life, he didn't get there by himself. I feel the same way.

Being led by the Holy Spirit, this book is a vivid example of the power of the Word, and how this 'turtle' ended up on the fence post of being published. More than eight years ago, still feeling the ache of grief in the loss of my wife, the first hint of this story came to me one morning during my time with the Lord. I can testify to the fact that the person of the Holy Spirit can speak through inspiration, prayer, Word, circumstance, music, etc., persistently, until you surrender to the guidance. Now, years later, this book is finished, and is more than a story; it is a resource in our personal faith journey along our respective Jericho Roads.

Over the years this book has been touched, caressed, shaped by the talent, the energy, and the faithful love of many. First, it was Beth Newcomer, author in her own right, who saw the power of the story and proceeded to practice editing tough love in the strengthening of the message.

Multiple editors have been involved in the manuscript. Each one contributing from the richness of their faith and experience. Lin Metzger has read significant parts of this story, at least twice; smoothing and gently challenging. Author Caryn Rivadeneira, of Honest Editing, polished and expressed her "love" for the story. Writer's Edge reviewed and called The Inn on Jericho Road a "Recommended Manuscript" placing it on their favored list.

The Chronology of Jesus' Ministry was developed and verified through Biblical studies and timelines from multiple sources over many years, and then completed by Robert Shepherd.

I am grateful to Kate Palazzi of faithQandA.com for the map of ancient Israel of Jesus' footsteps, on which I have identified, by number, the various points along Jesus' ministry.

My heart-felt thanks goes to my long-time friend, Dan Speicher, and the Speicher Family for their encouragement and support in the publication of this book.

It's with honor and praise that I express my gratitude to my Lord and Savior Jesus Christ whose Holy Spirit was there through each point along this Jericho Road journey, following the meaning and purpose of the Parable of the Good Samaritan. Honor and glory to Him. Amen.

Stan Escott

ABOUT THE AUTHOR:

Dr. Stanley (Stan) B. Escott, a retired professor with a PhD in Developmental Psychology, has a distinguished academic and pastoral background. His career spans over 45 years, with numerous roles including teacher, counselor, administrator, and lay pastor. Stan has contributed to juried academic journals, authored faith-based fiction books, and regularly shares his insights through weekly devotionals on his website, bosworth30.com. A lifelong Midwesterner, Stan has a fondness for Wyoming and Colorado. His family includes four children, seven grandchildren and five great-grandchildren, and one on the way. His book, *The Inn on Jericho Road*, reflects his experience and knowledge of the Christian experience.

Milton Keynes UK
Ingram Content Group UK Ltd.
UKHW042109131124
451149UK00006B/744